wild horses

ALBANY ARCHER

Copyright © 2024 by Albany Archer

All rights reserved.

This book is intended for your personal enjoyment. No part of this book may be reproduced in any form or by any electronic or mechanical means, without written permission from the author, except for the use of brief quotations and as permitted by U.S. copyright law.

This is a work of fiction.

E-book cover design by Chessa Anderson

Print cover design by Albany Archer via Canva

Editing: Tina Otero

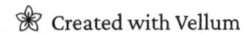

❀ Created with Vellum

Image from Anna Fury

WELCOME TO THE SEXY AS SIN SERIES,

where badass female athletes don't mind working up a good sweat on or off the field.

24 authors. 24 hot stories about fierce female athletes playing hard and finding love.

Bad boys. Good girls. City boys. Country girls. Enemies to lovers. Age gap. One-night stand. Second chances. Sweet and spicy. This collection of sexy novellas will have you cheering from the sidelines.

*to everyone who understands just how hard change can be.
and for those who think the saying should be wear the hat while the cowgirl rides you.*

introduction

Laramie

    Lucky Laramie Larson. I hate that nickname. I'm not lucky; I'm talented. And I'm not about to let a little thing like a torn rotator cuff keep me from my dream. It's delayed, not gone. Or that's what I tell myself as I work to get back into racing shape. I don't have time for distractions, especially not in the form of a pretty city boy like War Phillips.

    One night of fun. No strings. That's all it can be. So why do I regret sneaking out the next morning? And why does my heart jump when I run into War months later in the last place I expect?

War

    My seemingly perfect life is unraveling around me. The last thing I expect or need is Laramie Larson. I'm set on rebuilding my family and future; she's set on chasing wild horses across the country. Still, I can't resist her. Waking up alone the morning after the most incredible night of my life is a new low, but it's for the best. With Laramie gone, I can focus on making amends.

Running into her months later? Not on my bingo card. She's just as irresistible now as she was then, but her reckless ways burned me once. So why is my heart screaming that even though she might be trouble, she's also mine?

content notes

Please note, I have taken some liberties with the rodeo timeline and with the sport itself. I did my best to represent the spirit of barrel racing and the rodeo circuit, so please forgive any mistakes.

This book is an open-door romance, meaning there will be on page explicit sexual content: (not limited to) praise, back-door play, power exchange, and toy usage. Strong, descriptive language is used throughout, including during intimate encounters between the MCs.

Additionally, the book contains discussions and depictions of family estrangement, toxic family dynamics, mild injury, verbal harassment (not between MCs), and self-doubt.

Expect instalust and love. If these aren't your things, you probably won't enjoy this book. All spicy scenes are full of consent and eager enthusiasm. If you're interested in which chapters bring the heat, you can check out the dick-tionary in the back!

I've done my best to identify potential triggers, but if you see others, please let me know. Take care of your brain, your heart, and yourself!

CHAPTER ONE
Laramie

Waco, Texas
October

Expectation and excitement pebble across my skin as I breathe in. Leather. Saddle oil. Dust. Horsehair. The roar of the crowd. There's nothing in the world like the high of a rodeo.

A looped video of me tipping my hat and winking at the camera plays on the oversized screen while my name, ranking, and prior round times flash beneath my face. The packed arena hums with the buzz of the final-day crowd. Applause rains down, feeding the little goblin inside me who hungers for greatness, praise, and thrills.

"Laramie." The warm timbre of my dad's voice draws my attention. Squeezing my foot where it rests in the stirrup, he says, "You're up, kiddo. Run it clean," before disappearing into the crowd of rodeo hands.

Kit Larson is a man of few words, but he's never let me down. He can't make it to all my races now that I travel close to two-thirds of the year, but if I'm within a few hours, he's here.

I don't have to see him to know he's going to his seat so he can film my ride. It's the same thing he's done at every race he's been to since I was nine and decided being on the back of the fastest horse I could find was how I wanted to spend my life.

Comforted by the idea of him watching me, I shake out my shoulders, uncoiling the taut muscles. Despite almost two decades in the saddle, my nerves still flutter, and my stomach rolls. But I've learned to keep my hands steady and a smile on my face.

Like she owns the place, Xpresso struts into the alley. We wait near the gate handler, and I inhale once more. The familiar scents saturate my system. I count to five; then I exhale.

The chaos around me fades to black. No more knot in my gut. No more pulse ringing in my ears. No more applause. It's just me and the thousand pounds of animal between my thighs.

X is by far the best horse I've ever owned or ridden. She's been mine since she was a foal, and we've spent the last six years working toward this. Putting our time in, eating dirt, racing at rinky-dink local rodeos with no purse. Working circuit after circuit. Clawing our way up the rankings. Grinding as she grew into her talent, and I learned to read her like a book. Last year we were so close, seventeenth overall. Two spots away from the big show.

We were both disappointed. People are skeptical about what horses perceive, but X knew. She knew how close we came and how devastated I was when we were mere points from the top.

But that's okay. I pat her long neck as though she might read my thoughts and think I doubt her. I don't. This is our year. The season has been a dream. And winning tonight will clinch it—the proverbial feather in my ten-gallon hat.

X's ears flick, and she lets out a whinny. Anticipation burns through us both, so I lean forward, my voice calm. "I'm itching to go, too, but easy, girl. It's almost time." Tightening my grip on the saddle horn and the reins, X waits on my cue, her body—and mine—primed and ready to explode into motion.

Five.

My mind sharpens to a razor's edge.

Four.

The cloverleaf pattern is a brand in my brain. Three barrels stand between me and everything I've ever wanted.

Three.

I envision every turn, every stride X and I have to make to shave precious fractions of a second off the clock.

Two.

Sub-sixteen seals the deal.

One.

We can do it.

Go!

As one, we surge forward, bursting from the alley into the arena at a full gallop. Time doesn't cease to exist—it's all that matters—and we run on pure instinct. X and I deliver a masterclass in the delicate dance of speed and control. We race toward the first barrel as if our lives depend on it; less than half a minute seals our fate.

Just like my mental run-through, we're flawless. No stutters, no pauses. X's hooves thunder over the packed clay and loam, and together, we hug the turns like a Formula One driver let loose on an empty road.

As we round out the last barrel and shoot toward the straightaway, I can taste it. The buckle, the purse, the points. It's ours.

Rising in the saddle, I urge X on. "We've got this girl." Her mane and my long dark hair tangle together, our hearts beating in tandem, lungs gulping in air. We're two animals, one mind, Xpresso and I.

And we're going to win.

The open alley waits for us, the pathway to my dreams. Las Vegas. The national finals. All I have to do is reach out and take it.

My smile is beatific as we race past the finish line. I don't need to hear the announcer to confirm what I can feel in my bones. We did it.

Despite the adrenaline coursing through my veins, I ease up on the reins, guiding X to one of the designated cool-down lanes and taking her from a full-out gallop to a canter, then to a trot, and finally to a walk until we enter the holding pen. I dismount, and my sassy horse tosses her head, her chestnut mane flaring around her.

"You want me to braid your hair? Reward you for your hard work?" Her ears flick, and she nudges my pocket. "Ah, I see. You want peppermints." I snake one out and feed it to her as I loosen the cinch on the saddle.

A deep voice sounds behind me. "15.74."

With a whoop, I whirl around and, like I'm seven, jump into my dad's arms, bear-hugging the man who's supported me on each step of this journey. Through broken bones, broken spirits, and broken hearts. Through anxiety and disappointment. He isn't an emotional man, but I swear I see tears in his brown eyes.

"Proud of you, Mimi."

I hug him tighter at the use of my childhood nickname. "Love you, Dad."

"I wish your mom was here to see you now. She always was your biggest fan." He chuffs. "Well, second biggest."

Clearing his throat, my dad drops me to the ground. "Alright, enough of the mushy stuff." He tosses me my phone.

"I sent you the video of your run for you to review. Plus, you've got a horse to take care of." He studies me. "I'm heading to the trailer. You celebrating?"

Grinning, I shrug. He knows me well. The Barbie pink trailer I call home when on the road is comfy but confining, and I'm way too restless after a race—after a win—to bunk down for the night.

"Maybe a little." I pinch my thumb and index finger together and squint at him.

He kisses the top of my head. "Be safe. Be smart."

Be safe. Be smart. It's the same advice he's given me since he caught me at a party—in his stolen truck. He drove the tractor into town hunting for me, which, to my fourteen-year-old self, was the most embarrassing thing he could have done. He also grounded me for a month, but after that, I told him my plans. And he'd just say, "Be safe. Be smart."

I wish I could say I always heed his words, but more often than not, I chase sensation over security. Fast over slow. Surprise over steady. *Hence, the career riding on a horse racing around barrels.* I've given him more than a few gray hairs, but he's my rock.

Dad hugs me once more, then tips his hat and leaves. Snagging the reins, I guide X to the event stables. "Come on, girl, let's get you rubbed down and settled for the night. You deserve a couple of carrots. I might even have another peppermint for you."

Looping Xpresso's lead on a post, I make sure she has fresh straw and water, laughing when she walks in like the regal boss bitch she is. Then I take the saddle and gear off her before running my hands over her back and flanks, checking for any soreness or signs of irritation.

She swishes her tail in protest when my fingers run over a sensitive spot but otherwise stands still. She never shies away from letting me know what's bothering her, and for that I'm thankful. My well-being comes second to Xpresso's; she does the heavy lifting, after all. While she munches on a carrot, I inspect her hooves and remove the neoprene boots wrapped around her legs. Happy with everything, I brush her down, working her muscles, praising her. I fish a peppermint from my pocket and rest my forehead on her muzzle. "You kicked ass tonight."

Satisfied that Xpresso is good, I shut the stall door and take a deep breath. We fucking did it. They won't post official results for a while yet, but it's mine, ours—the National Finals Rodeo.

Letting out a loud cheer, I ignore the stares of the other riders around me. Not even the few annoyed glares coming my way can dampen this moment. Grinning like a fool, I straighten my hat, wash my hands, dust off my jeans, and make my way across the grounds. I wave to familiar faces and accept the congratulations tossed my way. A couple of the other racers I came up with from Juniors gather me in a big group hug, and I soak it in. Their support buoys my mood even more, and while we are competitive—we wouldn't be at this level if we weren't—their excitement for me is real.

Eventually, we split, the other ladies searching for their own ways to come down from the post-ride high. After a rodeo, there are all kinds of ways to let off steam. Sponsor parties, willing bed buddies, getting just this side of tipsy. My sponsors aren't the *host-a-party* type—being a mid-size tack company and my dad's stud farm—and I'm not in the mood for a quickie with any of the cowboys here. So tipsy it is.

I stop at a tent with a full cooler and a large spread of food. Snagging a beer, I let the hoppy flavor coat my tongue and wet my throat. It's exactly what I need. I finish the drink in minutes and snag three more. I load up a plate and do an internal happy dance when I find a table with room to spread out. Not that I need a lot; I'm pretty compact at five-four, but I like my space.

Music plays around me; someone's got a speaker hooked up, blaring stereotypical bro-country. Despite that, it's a perfect October night in Texas. The temp's on the right side of seventy, and a smattering of stars twinkle overhead. Nothing can spoil this day.

The second and third beers go down even smoother than the first. My muscles relax with each drink, and the hearty BBQ sandwich eases the annoyance of not eating all day. I nod and wave to another barrel racer sitting at the far end of the table. She smiles before her eyes widen, and she gathers her stuff, all but running away.

Seconds later, I understand why. The weight of the table shifts as two large bodies press in, one on my left and one on my right, just as Cyrus McClain plops down across from me. *Ah, not me she was running from then...*

"Nice ride tonight—for a dash dolly."

My shoulders rise to my ears at the dismissive term. Some cowboys on the circuit have a rage on for barrel racers. To them, we're spoiled, pampered princesses, relying on our daddies or boyfriends to finance a way to play dress up on a pony. Or worse, buckle chasers looking to snag the next PRCA champion. It's bullshit.

But it's also expected, so Cyrus' ugly words don't surprise me.

Taking a long draw from beer number four, I swallow. As flat as possible, I ask, "Need something?"

"Can't a friend offer congratulations?"

"A friend, yes. You? No. What do you really want?" The words come out harsh, but Cyrus McClain is *not* a friend. He's a misogynistic asshole. A creep. A loud drunk. A bully. A decent bronc buster. But a friend? No.

"Don't be like that." He clinks the lip of his bottle to mine. "Congrats on making it to Vegas, Lucky."

Lucky. Lucky Laramie Larson. Some announcer called me that years ago, and it stuck. I've spent every race since proving to the rodeo community luck has nothing to do with it. With a saccharine sweet smile, I say, "Not luck. Just talent. Something you wouldn't understand."

The man to my right chuckles until Cyrus shoots him a withering glare before saying, "Your horse does all the work, and you get all the glory. I'd like to see you stay on a bronc for longer than three seconds."

"Don't be mad you didn't make the leaderboard, McClain." This time, both men pinning me in cover their mouths to stifle their laughs.

Cyrus narrows his eyes. "You barrel bunnies walk around here like your shit don't stink. Like you're too good for guys like us."

By guys like us, do you mean incels? It takes great restraint, but I manage to swallow that thought.

I elbow the cowboys on either side of me, forcing some space between us as I stack my trash. I'm ready to be the bigger person and leave this conversation and the unwelcome company.

But then Cyrus goes and says four words I can't ignore. "You don't belong here."

The same inner voice that has me chasing thrills also serves as a pair of double devils on my shoulders when pushed too far. They've guided me at breakneck speeds down rocky cliffs. Literal and figurative. They were there in first grade when Brett Hoffman pulled my hair, and I knocked out his front tooth. Again, in junior high, when Shelby Johnson told everyone I stuffed my bra, so I flashed the room to prove I didn't. And for sure when my only long term boyfriend cheated on me, and I left his clothes on his front lawn, along with a not-so-subtle *fuck you* spray painted on his garage.

And those little devils are lighting a fire in me again. "Is that a challenge?"

"Oh, the bunny's got teeth." The swarthy cowboy to my left sneers.

Cyrus chuckles, but there's no warmth in it. "Naw, no challenge. Because there's no way you can hang. You're a typical arena princess. Hauling around that pink trailer in the pickup your daddy paid for. Riding on a ten-k pony, also paid for by your dad." He sniffs. "You're nothing but tits, ass, hair, and luck, Larson."

For the briefest moment, another voice breaks through—a quieter, calmer one.

Be safe. Be smart.

"Sorry, Dad," I mutter before downing the rest of my long neck and shoving up from the table, not caring when I knee goon two—Cyrus didn't bother introducing his companions to me, and I didn't bother to care—in the side. "I paid for X and that truck my own goddamn self. And even if he had paid for them, it wouldn't stop me from outlasting you. But then I imagine you're used to being outlasted in multiple areas of your life."

"How about you put that smart mouth to use, choking on my—"

I cut him off as he grabs his crotch. "I prefer foot longs to cocktail weenies, asshole. Now, are we doing this or not?"

Anger flashes on Cyrus' face as his buddies laugh. He shoots them a look that quiets them before raking his eyes over me from head to toe. His lecherous leer makes my Wranglers feel like a negligee. With a cruel smile, he says, "Let's see how lucky you are."

Five minutes later, I hoist myself over the gate that looks

out onto an empty practice arena. It's small, with packed dirt rather than the clay and loam mixture of the indoor facility. It's gonna hurt like a bitch if I fall, but I'm not backing down.

Goon two leads a stallion to the chute. The animal is agitated and annoyed. I don't blame him. I'd be grumpy if someone snatched me from the stock pen and brought me here.

Goon one tosses a saddle on the horse, who immediately bucks, fighting to toss it off. *Shit.* I ease closer to the chute, the raw power radiating off the stallion prickling over my skin. Am I really doing this? I've been around horses my entire life, but this is nothing like my usual ride.

Fueled by righteous indignation and beer number four, I steel my spine and mount up. The bronc snorts, stomps, and shudders, tossing his head. Doing my damnedest not to put too much tension on the flank strap, I tighten my grip and exhale.

The gate opens, and the horse explodes like a cannonball fired at an enemy ship. He's pure untamed energy, a frenzy of muscles and hooves. The initial burst jars the bones in my body, and I almost lose it right there. Each twist, kick, and buck requires every ounce of my strength to hang on. The reins are less than worthless even as the leather bites into my palm. My thighs scream as I use them to clench around the horse's sides.

An eternity passes until Goon One says, "I'll be damned—that's three."

Jubilant in my victory, I throw Cyrus a cocky smirk. And in that split second, that blink of an eye, my trajectory shifts. Something in my shoulder pulls, and a sudden, searing snap bursts in my muscles. My grip falters, the rein slipping as my arm goes numb and useless at my side.

Whatever small modicum of control I have over my body and the horse is gone, and the ground rises up to meet me.

From the dirt, I watch the bronc's dappled hindquarters race away while I struggle to draw air into my screaming lungs. As the world blurs around me, the sound of boots pounding toward me briefly cuts the haze, but then another wave of pain radiates outward from my right shoulder and down my arm. My wrist aches and my fingers tingle. I try to make a fist, try to keep my dream from slipping through my fingers, but I can't.

What the hell have I done?

CHAPTER TWO

war

Dallas, Texas
December

I stand in the doorway of my father's study, biting my tongue as he rakes my sister over the coals. Again.

Tuesday's anguished face is clearly displayed on the oversized screen mounted to the wall, dressed up like she's at a fundraiser or something—as are the others in the frame. Suits. Gowns. The ambient noise of partygoers. What catches my attention, though, are tears. Tears blurring eyes identical to my own.

Despite being twins, Tuesday and I have never been close. For thirty-three years, our parents manipulated us and found ways to pit us against each other. Even so, we tried to do what they asked, but Tuesday's effort has never been enough for them.

Meanwhile, I've benefited from this arrangement.

Tuesday's words to me when I called to check on her in October, when all this ugliness came to a massive head, echo in my mind. I hear them daily. *"You're right, War; we are family. I wish you'd kept that in mind before you determined I was worth less to you than the company... What I need right now is space and time. Please don't contact me."* My gut twists at all the ways I've let her down, hurt her. I don't begrudge her for wanting nothing to do with me.

Tuesday thinks I don't see how our parents, and my father in particular, treat her, but it's so much worse because I do. I've just been too much of a coward to defy him, and I hate myself for it. Our entire lives, I've played the role of the perfect Phillips heir. Backing my father's plays, putting my wants aside to learn the business and be everything he expects.

By nature, I'm a problem solver. It's my role in the company, and it's something I pride myself on. When that asshole, Duncan *fucking* Wright, managed to increase the disdain my father has for his daughter, I had to find a way to protect her.

Even though I knew she'd hate me and see it as a massive betrayal, sending Tuesday to Trail Creek, New Mexico *was* the correct choice. She needed to get out of Dallas, away from our parents and Duncan. Hell, away from me. There have always been bigger and better things waiting for Tuesday, and sending her to New Mexico helped her realize it. As days passed into weeks, I watched her from seven hundred miles away, using the snippets she posted on social media to keep track of her. And what I saw was my sister bloom.

But what I'm hearing tonight is too much. It's proof I haven't done enough.

My father's angry voice pulls me out of my head as he threatens to cut her off. The two volley back and forth; Tuesday balks and calls him out, but Warren Phillips ups the ante, promising to sell off the company we recently purchased from her new family.

Before I can speak up, a group surrounds my sister, a wall of support and love and everything I should be for her. The Davis family gave—gives—her things her blood family never has. As each person she's pulled into her light steps up, another boulder lodges in my chest, a heavy reminder of my failings. *You're a disgrace, War.*

Tuesday pleads with our father, offering to buy the company, promising to disappear. Then *Dad* says the words that break the dam inside me: "Your mistake is thinking I'd ever allow you a win."

The way he sees it, we're not his children—we're assets, leverage in his endless game. And god help anyone who tries to step off his board.

With a steadying breath and a quick whisper to the universe that my father buys what I'm selling, I move into the room, pushing past my parents. "Tuesday, I'll act as a proxy for you."

Shock flickers across my sister's face, replaced by a mix of hesitation and something that might be hope. Her hands, which had been wringing in her lap, freeze before she presses them together as if bracing herself.

"Wh-what? War, what are you saying? H-have you been there the entire time?" She falters, and the vulnerability of her words somehow cuts deeper than any of Dad's words ever could.

Ignoring my father's stern glare, I say, "I've been here long enough." And I don't just mean tonight.

My mother tuts from the expensive settee, her disapproval palpable. She doesn't need to say anything; the narrowing of her eyes is enough. Her support of my father's antics is quieter but no less poisonous, a reminder that her complicity in his unhinged plans means Tuesday and I only have each other— and I've left her alone for years.

The entire situation would be absurd, like something out of a soap opera, if it weren't so disgusting. Our father agreeing to pay Duncan Wright, the lying, manipulative asshole who threatened to sue our company, a million dollars is bad enough. Trying to marry Tuesday off to him after he violated her privacy and attempted to blackmail her—all to salvage the company's reputation and save face among his peers—is even worse. But never in all my imagined worst case scenarios and worst *worst* case scenarios did I see my father sending that prick to Trail Creek to try and make Tuesday come home.

Dropping by my parents' house was pure coincidence, but I'm thankful for it. Who knows when I would have heard Mom and Dad's twisted version of what's happening here tonight.

As always, it comes down to money and image with Warren Phillips. He's used both to twist and mold Tuesday and me into a caricature of a family. He cares more about what people think and his bottom line than he does for either of us. I've always been a better pawn than Tuesday, willingly shuffled along at his whim.

She's so much braver than me. Seeing her hold her ground against our father reinforces that.

Tuesday's nose wrinkles. "War, you can't act as my proxy, and you know it. They'll never let you." Is she saying this to urge me on or preparing for me to crumble under the pressure?

"Don't worry about me." Doubt pools in my gut despite the confidence I'm projecting. Can I pull this off? If I fail her again, I'll never forgive myself.

My father's voice, ice cold, slips over me. "War, what's gotten into you? You dare turn your back on your mother and me? On the company? After all I've given you?"

Straightening my tie, I smirk, letting the warmth leave my eyes. I put every bit of conviction I possess into my words.

"Don't take it personally, Dad; it makes perfect sense from the business side. I've already messaged my idea to several board members, and they love it." I get entirely too much pleasure from the way the color drains from my father's face.

And yet, it doesn't feel like the victory it should. It's one thing to fight him with the weapons he taught me—manipulation and leverage—but what does it say about me that I can wield them so effortlessly? Shit, maybe I'm more like him than I want to admit.

"What idea?"

"To sell Davis Designs back to the Davis family with Tuesday as the purchaser."

"Why would you do that?" He sounds like the snake he is, the words hissed from between clenched teeth.

I have to convince him I have the necessary votes in my pocket. Without missing a beat, I say, "Some of the more vocal shareholders are less than thrilled about bringing a person who sued our company back into the fold."

Dad blanches, then barks, "How would they know about that?"

Outside, I'm nonchalant, but this is it. He'll either buy the story—and for once, Tuesday will get the win she deserves—or he'll call my bluff, and I'll fail her again.

I dust a nonexistent piece of lint from the cuff of my jacket. "Perhaps someone let it slip that you and Duncan came to a less-than-savory, off-the-books agreement. Maybe that same someone raised concerns that we stretched ourselves too thin expanding into neighboring states and that it would be best for our ROI if we refocused on our local market." Dropping the bored tone, I let an ounce of the anger that's festered in me for years break through. "And who better to purchase our failed out-of-state venture than your daughter? Spreading her wings with the approval of her..." The next words taste bitter, like the lie they are. "Loving father. It's a compelling story."

From the screen, I hear a snort. Tuesday knows how much bullshit I'm spouting right now, but I can't let it derail my momentum. Coughing to cover a laugh, I say, "At a ten percent increase, of course."

"Of course," Tuesday readily agrees, a smile tugging at her lips along with a flicker of something. Gratitude? She's so used to standing alone against our parents; it's no wonder she doesn't know how to process me standing with her.

It's dangerous, lying about already having board members on my side, but Dad is cracking. And when I *do* disclose what he's done, the board *will* be on my side. I won't let his ego and warped sense of family hurt Tuesday anymore, and if I have to pull a thousand strings, owe a thousand favors to make this go through, then that's what I'll do.

With a wave of anger I'm sure to feel the wrath of for months to come, my father storms from the room, my mother in his wake. I can't pretend I care. Instead, I give my attention to the one person I should have been here for—the person I've let down and hurt more than anyone else.

I'm more than ready to balance the scale I've let tip out of whack. I owe her years' worth of amends.

"Tuesday, Trail Creek looks good on you. It's nice to see you with so many people who love you." I mean it; she looks settled. A stab of jealousy flickers in my chest. *I want that.*

"Thank you. How did you do this? And why?" she asks quietly, her question simple but weighted.

Swallowing, I think of the answer I gave Bond Davis, the man who loves my sister, when he asked me a similar question. "Sometimes families make difficult choices that are hard to explain—"

"But truly are in everyone's best interest," Bond and his father, Scott, finish.

The people who have become the family she deserves study me through Tuesday's phone camera, their piercing stares cutting the distance between us to nothing. Leaning into the camera and covering my discomfort, I say, "What they said. And don't worry about Mom and Dad. I'll ensure the board accepts your offer, and they'll be pretending none of this ever happened before the ink dries on the contract." I will make this happen for her, no matter what it costs.

"Thank you, War." Tuesday hesitates, her voice hitching as if unsure of her next words. "It might be nice if you came and visited. See why I love it here so much."

My heart aches, and I quirk my lips in a half-smile. "I may take you up on that." She doesn't mean it, though. Not really. Not yet. But I planted a seed tonight. One I can hopefully help grow into more. I've missed out on so much. I don't want to miss her wedding. The chance to be Uncle War. The chance to get to know my sister.

I slump into my father's chair, staring at the now-empty screen. The truth is, I've always envied Tuesday, not for her struggles but for her courage. Helping her now feels like the start of making amends, but maybe it's selfish. Am I doing this for her or me?

The thought gnaws at me, and I push it aside, grabbing a scotch from the cabinet and granting myself a healthy pour. I just fired the first shot, and I'm smart enough to know Warren Phillips won't take it lying down. Tonight, I'll let the alcohol dull the *what-ifs* swirling in my head. Tomorrow, I'll deal with the fallout.

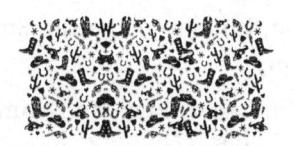

I focus on my form as I slice through the water like a blade. The last few days have been fraught with behind-the-scenes negotiation and promise-making to square away the deal I made with Tuesday, but it's worth it. Getting everything settled for her is a small drop on the positive side of my karmic balance.

The board members and shareholders were less than impressed with Dad's plan to bring Duncan back after the shit he pulled. They were, thankfully, content with the increase in the sale price. My father has been a spiteful dick, but I expected it. We've been locked in a brutal battle since the night I snaked Davis Designs out from under him. *And supported Tuesday.*

He's threatened to fire me, disown me, and more. I'm getting a small taste of what Tuesday dealt with for years. Outright disdain, hostility, and snide comments about how much of a disappointment I am.

God, I'm such a fuck up. I should have stood up for her so long ago, but it was easier to keep my blinders on and pretend we were the happy family our parents paraded before shareholders and the Dallas elite. To fall into the role my parents expected me to play. I wore the mask well, and despite it being suffocating, I refused to remove it. But now that I have, I can see so much more.

Pushing my body, I swim faster. This is the only time my head clears, the only place I've ever found peace. I swam throughout high school and college. My parents allowed it because it looked good to have an athlete in the family, but once I graduated, my father did everything he could to squash my enjoyment of the sport. Reminded me of how time away from work was time wasted, and if I was going to take over

Phillips Construction, I had to be better. Smarter. The biggest shark in a sea of them.

Today, though, I'm where I belong. Swimming like it hasn't been ten years since I last trained. Swimming like my life depends on it. Harder than I ever pushed myself in a race. If I move faster, can I outrun my guilt and failures? My loneliness? Can the chlorinated water dilute my memories?

It's funny how clarity can make you look back and realize how foolish you've been. Hindsight and all that. I've spent thirty-three years going through the motions of a life that is perfect on paper. Years being my father's yes-man. The tailored suits, the corner office, the six-figure career—none of it matters. Not when I go home to an empty apartment, drink alone, and wonder if anyone would notice if I didn't show up tomorrow.

I flip under the water, kick off the wall, and push myself beyond my limits. This is supposed to clear my head, not mire me deeper. *Swim faster. Push harder. Outrun the thoughts.*

What if I'd stood up for Tuesday years ago? My shoulders and thighs scream, but I press on, the laps endless as I work the self-loathing and doubts out of my body.

Lap thirty.

Would I be stuck fighting for a share of a *family* business I'm not sure I want? I suck in ragged gasps, and my left shoulder throbs, impacting my stroke.

Lap thirty-five.

Would I have more than a shattered relationship with my only sibling? My lungs burn, and my arms are leaden, but stopping is surrender. So, despite the discomfort, I push.

Lap forty.

The water isn't washing away my guilt; no, it's drowning me in it. Then, with one wrong pull, pain, sharp and searing, radiates down my arm. I grit my teeth, stubbornly refusing to give up.

One more stroke. One more lap.

It's too much to fight, and I slow, drifting to the wall, chest heaving as I clutch my shoulder. Just a strain, I tell myself, as I knead the muscle. Hauling myself from the water takes three times as long as it should, and it's then I know I'm going to need more than some ibuprofen and a good night's sleep to shake this off.

But it's no less than I deserve.

CHAPTER THREE
Laramie

Dallas, Texas
December

A very unladylike grunt slips between my lips as I glare at the five-pound dumbbell acting as the bane of my existence. How something so small, so inconsequential, can reduce me to such failure is baffling. When I try—and again fail—to lift the weight higher than ninety degrees, I drop it with a curse. Then kick it further away for good measure.

It only hurts a lot. "Stupid motherfu—"

"What did that weight ever do to you?"

My eyes dart to the handsome man using the little arm bike thing. He shoots me a smile that would have a nun loosening her habit and I duck my head, looking away. This is the second physical therapy session he and I have shared, and while we spent the last one eye-flirting, I don't have time for distractions today. Not when my entire career hangs by a thread.

He is an excellent distraction, though. Especially the way

his biceps tighten and the veins in his forearms flex... *Nope. Stop that right now.*

Shaking off my lust-fueled haze, I grumble, "Why don't you peddle yourself right on outta here, Pretty Boy?"

"Pretty Boy?" He arches an eyebrow and rubs the stubble along his chiseled jawline. Not that I'm staring or anything.

"I can see it, Mr. Phillips. Now move those arms." Dr. Panter startles me; I'm so busy drowning in Pretty Boy's honey-brown eyes that I don't notice her until she's right next to me. And considering the reindeer antlers on her head, that's saying something.

"War, Dr. Panter. Please call me War. Mr. Phillips is *absolutely* my father." His deep tenor sours. Part of me wants to be nosy and ask what that's about, but I have bigger things going on than prying into some random hottie's business.

Dr. Panter waves at the man, War, and directs him back to his slow hand peddling. To me, she pats the padded therapy table.

Like a good patient, I hop up, mainly because I know I'm about to get scolded.

"Why are the free weights already out, Ms. Larson?"

I roll my shoulder as Dr. Panter watches, waiting. The dull throb I've learned to live with since October is there, a persistent reminder of my dumbassery.

Why did I pick up the weight first? Because it's nothing. It's five pounds. I've spent my life hauling bags of feed, saddles, and tack, shoveling out stalls, climbing fences and trees, and riding nine-hundred-pound animals. All of which require way more strength than simply lifting a five-fucking-pound weight.

"Oh, I got those out," War says, still peddling his way to nowhere with his arms.

"You didn't, but it's admirable of you to lie for Ms. Larson." Dr. Panter doesn't take her discerning stare off me.

A smile tugs at my lips. "Thanks for trying to cover for me, Pretty Boy." Louder, I add, "Laramie. Please call me Laramie."

While I say the words to Dr. Panter, she rolls her eyes and smiles. "Yes, I'm aware, *Laramie*, given I've been seeing you every Tuesday and Thursday for the past three weeks. Now, let's get you warmed up. Then you can work on lifts."

She moves me through a series of steady, *slow*, smooth movements. Only when I'm panting through gritted teeth and my shoulder burns does Dr. Panter offer me the tiny purple weight.

With all the determination I possess, I grip the weight, the small item deceptively heavy in my fist. My arm trembles as I raise it, not even making it to shoulder height. The pulling, twisting sensation makes my teeth clench. Tension pulls the muscles like rubber bands stretched too tight. It's not just painful—it's wrong. This isn't the burn of a challenging workout; it's the bite of overexertion, the wrench of scar tissue, and it's almost enough to make me quit.

I lower the weight and repeat, but this time, I rotate my arm before slowly moving it outward. It hurts. There's no other way to say it. Each tiny motion sends waves of agony through my shoulder, pulling at the place where the surgery stitched me back together. My muscles spasm in revolt, and my arm falls limp.

A dark, angry part of me relishes the burn. Yes, being able to do these movements at all is a good thing, but I deserve the hurt that comes with it.

It's been seven weeks since the *minor* surgery to repair the *minor* tear in my rotator cuff, and I'm itching to get back in Xpresso's saddle. But given I can't even lift a five-pound weight higher than ninety degrees, the chance of my being able to ride my horse with the precision I expect is slim to none. So, instead of celebrating in Vegas, I'm stuck in Dallas.

The finals. My finals. I should be there. *I was there.* Everything I wanted was in my hands, and like a reckless idiot, I threw it away to prove a point to Cyrus fucking McClain.

Another groan of pain and frustration fills the open therapy room. Other PT patients, including War, give me a side-eye. If I weren't trying to pretend that this minuscule hand weight wasn't Sisyphus' stone, I'd flip them off. Or, in War's case, maybe blow a kiss.

He really is good-looking. Tall, trim, a little too clean-cut. His reddish-brown hair and those warm eyes—not unlike a chestnut stallion—definitely have appeal. Yes, that man would look mighty fine grazing in my pasture.

Biting my lip, I shake the image of War's broad shoulders between my thighs from my head and refocus on lifting the weight. Refocus on why I'm here.

Turning my attention to the large whiteboard, I search until I find my initials written in neat handwriting with a list of goals. Sitting at number one? Compete in the High Plains Stampede. Slightly lower on the list—pat the top of my head. Dr. Panter says it's important to have a wide range of objectives.

High Plains isn't a huge event, but it's big enough to make a statement. Most of the circuit will be there, thick in the swing of things. I picked it purposefully. When I return, I want everyone to remember why they should be worried.

The petty side of me refuses to watch the finals. It's too tender a wound. When Dad asked if I wanted updates, I threatened to eat the stuffing from his Oreos if he spilled a word about it. I'll find out soon enough, anyway.

My competition is out there now, either shining under the bright Vegas lights or resting and regrouping, mentally planning how to take the buckle, the crown, the title. Meanwhile, I'm struggling to lift the same weight my Memaw uses in her seventies-plus aerobics class. The thought of missing out on the finals—again—gnaws at my stomach, leaving a gaping hollow. What if I can't come back from this? What if this is the new me? A weak, broken version of myself?

Lost in my thoughts, I lift my arm too high, twist it too fast, and the ache in my shoulder grows into a white-hot flare that shoots down my arm. My entire shoulder spasms and the weight falls to the ground. If I was a crier, I'd be fighting tears. Instead, I cuss a storm of words that would've had my mom washing my mouth out with soap.

War lurches forward as if coming my way, but before he can untangle himself from the pulley he's currently working at, Dr. Panter's cool hands settle on my shoulder.

"Laramie, breathe. It's okay to take it down a notch," she says as she kneads the muscle. "This isn't about pushing as hard as you can. It's about getting to where you were safely. Progress, even if it feels slow, is progress."

Sighing, I say, "I wish it wasn't so out of my control. My mind says I can, but my body..."

"In this case, listen to your body." Dr. Panter works my arm, stretching and tugging. With each pass, she pulls my hand higher and higher. We're at ninety degrees, and I know what's coming. Biting the inside of my cheek to keep from making a noise, I prepare myself for the discomfort at the incision site—the pull deep in my shoulder blade.

I squeeze my eyes shut and pretend I'm somewhere else—in a bar kissing the corded muscles of War's neck, maybe—as she pushes my arm to the side. My wrist is almost even with my ear when I can't take anymore, and I jerk away from her grip.

"Easy, Laramie. You did great. I know you're frustrated, but you're making remarkable progress. Now, I want you to do wall presses and scapular retractions, then hit the hot tub."

As much as I don't want to do any more exercises, I'm totally on board with the hot tub. "No ice bath?"

Dr. Panter's lips quirk. "Nope, you're spared the trauma of the ice today. I'll see you Thursday."

Giving my thanks, I set to it. Warm, bubbly water and a chance to unwind are calling my name.

By the time I finish the last set of *scapular retractions,* aka squeezing my shoulder blades together until I want to cry, the PT room is empty except for War and Dr. Panter. Nodding my goodbye to them, I push into the small changing room and slip into the functional one-piece I bought for aqua therapy. *Doesn't matter if it's flattering, Laramie.* Does a piece of me wish it was a cute bikini? And that a certain someone was joining me in the water?

Giving myself a mental slap, I push War and his handsome face from my mind. I swear my hormones are out of whack. I haven't had a satisfying orgasm since before my accident. That's all this crush is—the need to get laid.

Tinkling holiday music plays over the speakers, mixing with the bubbling of the jets and swishing of the lap pool. The sun sets behind the Dallas skyline, leaving the room bathed in soft shades. The faint scent of chlorine tickles my nose when I step into the hot tub, and I sigh as the warm water and pulse of the jets work my sore muscles. The heat wraps around my aching shoulder, and while it dulls the persistent throb, it does nothing to quiet my restless mind.

The memory of my last race replays in my head in hi-def: the high is intoxicating as X and I race, rounding each barrel so perfectly—the promise of a win in my grasp. Then, the scene changes, and I'm on my back in a red clay arena, staring up at the sky, unable to breathe. I rub my hand over my shoulder, the small scar hidden by my swimsuit a reminder of all I lost. Of my mistakes.

Regret and anger—at myself, at Cyrus, at the universe—knot together in a tangle of frustration inside me. I sink lower in the water until my ears are submerged, muffling the holiday music. Then deeper, until the entire world disappears. If I stay submerged long enough, can I drown the what-ifs swirling in my head?

Suddenly, a large hand yanks me upward, and I jolt, sputtering and coughing.

"Are you okay? Jesus, Trouble, you scared me."

"Wh-what?" I swipe away the stinging water blurring everything around me. A shape shifts in front of me. Blinking harder, I focus on the figure until it crystalizes into the bare chest of a man. A bare *broad* chest with a smattering of reddish-brown hair that tapers off before picking up below his navel. *Shit, Laramie, stop ogling the man.* I force my eyes upward.

War leans over me, concern etched on his brow. "You were under the water when I came in."

"Did you call me Trouble?" I ask, not sure what I'm saying.

"I did. You've got it written all over you." War smiles. "Mind if I join you?" When I don't immediately answer him, his grin falters. "Or not."

I grab his hand, shuddering at the spark my skin against his generates. "No, I mean, yes. Join me."

"What were you doing underwater?" War asks, sliding into the hot tub. He's close enough that our knees touch.

What was I doing? Reliving one of the stupidest decisions I've ever made. Remembering how I couldn't catch my breath. "Meditation."

He purses his lips. "You don't seem like the meditating type."

"I'm totally Zen. Plus, it's not like you know me, Pretty Boy." I nudge his shoulder with mine, ducking my head when we both wince.

"The way you kicked that weight earlier and cussed like a sailor says otherwise."

"Okay, maybe I'm still mastering the art of tranquility." He shoots me a devastating smile before we fall into silence. The quiet between us shifts from comfortable to awkward, and I can't help but break it. "So, what're you in for?" *Ugh, nice, Laramie. You make it sound like we're doing time, not soaking in a hot tub at a bespoke physical therapy center.*

If War is put off by my phrasing, he doesn't show it. "Swimming injury. Or maybe a being-over-thirty injury."

"Ah, so you're an old man."

He arches one eyebrow. "Thirty-three isn't old."

"If you're telling me in six years I'll be back here because of swimming, I have to disagree with you."

"You're a little bit of a smartass, aren't you?" His words are softened by his teasing grin.

I pinch my fingers together. "A little."

The back and forth comes naturally, and I can't help but notice War's gaze lingering on my lips a fraction too long to be innocent. A shiver of lust licks down my spine.

Shaking his head, War clears his throat, then asks, "What about you? How'd you end up here? Pilates?"

My nose wrinkles. "Pilates? That's the vibe I give off?"

"Okay." He lets out a rumbly laugh. "Not pilates. So what then?"

"Got bucked off a bronco."

"You're kidding?" His eyes widen.

"Nope."

"Damn, you really are trouble, aren't you?"

"You have no idea, Pretty Boy."

War inches closer, his fingers brushing against my thigh. "You're right, I don't. But that sounds like a fixable problem." His voice is soft but sure, and for a split second, I wonder what his lips would feel like on mine.

I let out a low, throaty laugh. "Good luck with that."

We lean in as if drawn by some unseen force, but whatever might happen comes to a screeching halt as the door swings open, shattering the moment.

"Hey, folks, we're closing." The staff member in her crisp polo looks at us expectantly.

War rises, and I stare a little too long at the water sluicing down his torso. His hand reaching for mine breaks me out of my stupor. He helps me out of the hot tub and snags a towel, gently wrapping it around my shoulders. Leaning forward, his lips graze my ear. "I'm a problem solver, Laramie, and learning more about you is on my list now."

I gulp, tingles of desire coursing through me.

With a knowing smirk, War winks. "See you Thursday, Trouble."

CHAPTER FOUR

war

I fiddle with my watch, the large rose-gold cage glinting as I triple-check the time. Since starting physical therapy, I've never been in a hurry to get there. Today, though, a current of urgency spurs me forward that has nothing to do with the brisk December air. It's funny how something as simple as meeting a beautiful woman can change your perspective. Knowing I'll see Laramie today—and hopefully learn more about her—is an unexpected bright spot.

She waltzed into Dr. Panter's office like she owned the place, a natural swagger to her steps that captured my attention. We spent that entire first session staring at each other across the room, and even though we didn't speak, it was the best foreplay I've had in a long while—to the point I had to take matters into my own hands when I got home. I didn't even know her name then, but the idea of that lithe body riding mine is an image I still can't shake.

Then, at our next shared session, I got to talk with her. Her husky drawl drew me in, as did her colorful language. Who knew someone cussing out a dumbbell could be adorable? I found myself lying for her and wanting to help her when she was hurting. When I walked into the aquatic therapy room and found her below the water's surface in the hot tub, a surge of protectiveness and panic flared in me. Maybe standing up for Tuesday awoke some long-dormant instincts, but everything in me screamed to grab her and make sure she was okay.

There's a magnetic force around Laramie, and it's put me on a trajectory straight into her orbit.

It's not like I haven't dated over the years, but most of those were orchestrated interactions with *socially acceptable* women brought forth by my parents and their equally shallow friends. I've never had an immediate, instant attraction to another person like what I feel now. Everything about Laramie calls to me, despite knowing nothing about her.

Hell, maybe that's *why* she appeals to me. She's an unknown. Not a polished Pilates princess or a spoiled debutante hand-picked by my parents for her background and status. There's something inherently untamed about her, something wild. Something that demands I let it pull me along.

Shaking my head, I dismiss my thoughts. This is stress and lust talking. It's been way too long since I got laid. Nothing more. I pick up my pace, wanting to make sure I get to PT on time—for my health and no other reason—when my phone buzzes.

> **TUESDAY**
>
> Heads up. Mom and Dad have been calling my lawyers around the clock. Making some pretty big threats.

I stop in the middle of the sidewalk, grunting out an apology to the man who crashes into my shoulder. Aggravation coils with physical pain as I reread my sister's text. I hurriedly pull up all my documentation, confirming everything, before replying.

> Davis Designs is safe. The new contract is bulletproof. You don't need to worry.

> But do you?

All it takes are three words to remind me of the difference between Tuesday and myself. Her concern for me comes through despite my not having done enough to earn it.

My phone rings, and my father's information pops up on the screen. My muscle memory goes to answer until my newfound spine has me swiping ignore.

> I'm not worried. No matter what happens. I did the right thing.

> For once ☺

Tuesday hearts my message, and I grant myself a smile. I'll take that little digital heart. It's another brick in the relationship we're slowly rebuilding. We've texted more over the past few days than we have in years. Me, assuring her everything is going to plan here in Dallas. Her, sharing small, superficial snippets of her life in New Mexico.

My grin grows thinking of the pictures she sent yesterday of herself and her friends eating massive croissants drizzled with honey in a cute bakery. *I bet Laramie likes croissants. And honey...* My phone rings again, pulling me from the image of licking crumbs off a certain brunette's lips.

Fuck. It's Dad again. The twinge in my shoulder, the cold, and now phone calls from my father. None of these things are helping my mood.

I answer the phone in a clipped but professional tone, the

one I've perfected over the years. "Hello, Father. How are you?" I'm still on the street, a block from Dr. Panter's office, but I want this conversation done before I get there.

The chilly December wind howling between the Dallas skyscrapers has nothing on the ice in my father's voice. "I warned you what would happen if you followed through with helping your sister. Did you think I was joking?"

Huffing, I pinch the bridge of my nose. "No, and you've made it clear every day since. Do you have something new to say, or are you just going to bark the same toothless threats each time we speak?"

"Watch yourself, Warren. I'm still the majority shareholder of this company. The company *I* built. One call to HR and you're out. Your job is on the line as it is."

My job. *Vice President of Business Development.* Aka, my father's second banana, overseeing the securing of new contracts and client relationships and perceptions. Perceptions. They are all that matter to him. And for so long, they were all that mattered to me, too. For the hundredth time since sending Tuesday to Trail Creek, I wonder why.

"Warren!" His shout of my name is sharp and cutting.

"Sir?" I curse myself for the automatic reply.

He chuffs, then says, "All you have to do is set this right. A quick shareholder meeting, apologizing for the... ugliness of the situation, and we can put this behind us. It may say Phillips Construction, but that doesn't mean the company has to stay in the family."

Disowning me and keeping the company from me have become his go-tos. It's becoming clear, as I refuse to come to heel, he has no idea how to approach me. His word has always been law, but the more I defy him, the more his weakness shines. Putting a smirk into my words, I say, "Family? It's funny you'd call us that."

In the background, my mother's appalled voice sounds. "Warren, of course, we are a family. Think of how much your father and I have done for you."

This, more than anything else, tests my temper. "Here's what you've done for me. You've shown me how to manipulate people, how to bulldoze and bully my way into getting what I want. How to never treat my own children." I pause and let out a mirthless chuckle. "I should thank you for that last one."

"Apologize to your mother. Now." The heat and anger in my father's words would have blistered me in the past; now, they simply warm my bones.

"No, I don't think I will. It's you who should apologize, *sir*." I put years' worth of disdain and disillusionment into the honorific. "You were and are wrong, and I'm done standing by while you alienate and abuse my sister."

My mother's scandalized gasp has me rubbing my temples. How did I let things get to this point? How was I so blind to their true natures?

"Don't worry, Mother. No one is around to hear the conversation on my end. I know that's what you're actually concerned about. And it is abuse. Emotional, at least. I just hate that it took me so long to wake up. You're goddamn wrong for it, but so am I for not protecting Tuesday years ago." Guilt eats at me, and I rub the heel of my hand against my sternum. "Do what you will. Cut me off, remove me from the company. I don't care."

The words are out of my mouth before my brain can process what I've said. I wait for regret. Panic. Fear. Instead, there's a lightness, an easing of the rock in my chest and tension in my shoulders. It's a startling realization to find I mean what I said. *I don't care.*

For the first time in my life, apart from the night I stood up for Tuesday, I genuinely don't care what my parents think.

"You're making a mistake. Mark my words, son."

I can't stop the scoff that slips from my throat. "Let me be clear: whatever control you've had over me is done. I'm not afraid to stand on my own. I'm smart, capable, and have a tidy bank account. There's nothing you can hold over me."

Shedding the weight of my parents' expectations is easier than I ever dreamed. Why didn't I do this years ago? For so long, I've convinced myself I wanted this life, to take over Phillips Construction and be the man my parents molded me to be.

Is this how Tuesday feels? No wonder she never wants to leave Trail Creek.

"This conversation is not over, Warren. If you think you can simply dismiss your mother and me this way, you're sorely mistaken. I'll make it so no one in the metroplex will touch you. If there's no one to do business with, then you can't branch out on your own. How will you find contractors and suppliers? Do you think they'd forfeit my business to take a chance with you?"

My harsh laugh sounds brittle. "I hope one day you grasp what you've done. How far you've pushed your children, to the point you have nothing and no one left."

With nothing else to say, I hang up, send one last text to Tuesday in case our parents reach out to her directly, then put my phone on Do Not Disturb. My palms are sweaty, and I'd probably set off alarms if someone measured my blood pressure, but I fucking did it.

I parse through my father's threats. They aren't idle; I know that much. I've observed from the wings as Warren Phillips crushed competitors with smear campaigns and blackball tactics. Leveraging his multi-million-dollar business to crowd out the market. But it's oddly relieving. I don't want to take over Phillips Construction. I don't want to do anything with construction.

What do I want? That's a question I can't answer yet, but the thought of unemployment isn't as frightening as I expected. A glance at my watch has me jogging toward Dr. Panter's office. The ramifications of what I've done can wait. I've got a PT session, a cute-as-hell cowgirl, and my entire future waiting for me.

CHAPTER FIVE
Laramie

I not-so-subtly crane my head, once again searching over the empty machines and unfamiliar faces around me. It's ten minutes into the time slot War and I share, but he's a no-show. As more time passes, the sour feeling in my stomach intensifies. Where is he?

Something light and fluffy sets loose in my chest when I spy broad shoulders, ending in a tapered waist. That same something instantly flitters away when I realize the hair is too dark, the arms not quite as toned.

Ugh. What the hell am I doing? I should *not* be scanning the room for a glint of red in a head of light brown hair. Wondering why he's late. If he's going to show. No, I should concentrate on my exercises. Not remembering War's parting words about him being a problem solver, and how they stuck with me for way longer than they should have. As in over multiple self-induced orgasms and fantasies.

Scolding myself, I go back to my shoulder lifts. *Get it together, Laramie.* Physical therapy is not the place for some meet-cute with my other half.

I'm here for one reason: to regain my strength so I can compete again. To salvage what I lost. The last thing I need is a delicious distraction, like War Phillips, keeping me from being one hundred percent focused on my goals.

"So, Laramie, how are you today?"

My heart skips a beat. I swear, Dr. Panter needs a bell.

"Um, not too bad, but I haven't plunged into the wonderful world of scapular retractions yet."

She gives me an indulgent smile. "Yes. I'm quite the taskmaster, aren't I? But you're here for a reason."

"Because you're the best."

"Because I'm the best. All the soreness and seeming setbacks will be worth it in the end. I promise, if you keep putting in the work, you will be back to where you were in time for your March competition." She pauses, serious black eyes narrowing. "Though I wish I could talk you into a less dangerous goal. I don't want you back here a year from now. Which is also why it's important to pace yourself and put *all* your attention into getting better."

It's like she senses how split my concentration is. Pieces of it siphoned away by a chiseled jaw and wide shoulders.

As if thinking of him summons him from the ether, War is there, his warm honey-brown eyes locking on mine as a slight grin plays on his full lips. It's unfair how pretty he is. A bubbling, buoyant sensation and a sudden rush of heat spread through me. Did someone turn the temperature up in here?

"Ah, Mr. Phillips, how nice of you to join us. You're late." Dr. Panter scolds him like he's a wayward child.

War runs a hand through his hair, mussing the neat strands. "Please, Dr. Panter, I'm begging you, call me War. And I'm sorry; I had a personal matter to attend to." A flash of something, hurt maybe, flickers across his face before disappearing. "It won't happen again."

Dr. Panter nods. "Alright, let's get you started then. Laramie, you know what to do. I'll check your progress in a bit."

I watch War move to one of the cardio stations, appreciating how his tapered joggers and tight-fitting t-shirt cling to his toned body. Damn this handsome man. He wields entirely too much power over my brain.

It's been over a year since I've dated anyone, and for good reason. Men are turds. Of course, there are good ones out there—my dad and Ted Lasso, for example—but as a majority? Turds.

Is War Phillips a good one? I tilt my head, trying to study him without getting caught. Physically? He's very, very good. Broad and trim. Tall with big hands. But emotionally? Who knows?

My instincts, my twin devils, shout at me to take him for a ride. However, those little bastards are also the ones who led me to this point. I wouldn't be rehabbing a busted shoulder if I hadn't listened to them.

But I also wouldn't have half the fun I've had without those instincts, and I *really* love fun.

One night. One night of kissing and tasting and entwining my body with his. One night to work him out of my system. People do that, right? Granted, in every romance book I've ever read, once is never enough, but that's fiction. This is real life.

Plus, I'm not built for more. My last relationship—if one date at the local Dairy Queen and a night making out in a pickup qualify as a relationship—ended when I beat his younger sister's qualifying time. The one before that was two dates with a *Done in 60 Seconds* fella, and I prefer more staying power. Or at least a reciprocal offering... And before that was the cheater. My track record speaks for itself.

No, relationships and Laramie Larson do not mix, and

despite not even knowing the guy, I get the feeling my Pretty Boy is looking for more than a quick lay.

Blowing an errant hair out of my eye, I give myself a mental slap.

Laramie, get your shit together.

I refocus on my weights. Well, I mostly refocus on my weights. Okay, fifty-one percent of me totally focuses on the weights. The traitorous other forty-nine percent is busy drooling over the sweat dripping down the column of War's throat.

Guess it's a good thing I can multitask—

I'm busted as soon as the dumbbell slips from my grip and hits the ground. Dr. Panter and War's heads snap in my direction, one tight with concern, the other with a shake of her head. War takes a step forward; this man is always half-rushing to my aid. It's like he's part white knight but only just got his horse and has no clue what to do with his shield.

Dr. Panter points to a massage table. "Go to the massage table, Laramie."

Sufficiently embarrassed, I skulk behind Dr. Panter to the furthest corner of the PT room and haul myself up on the padded table.

"There are," she pauses and waves, "distractions everywhere. My job is to give you the tools to rebuild your body. Your job is to let me, and that means giving it your all when you're here." She lowers her voice. "He is handsome, but I can't have you injuring yourself. It's not safe if you aren't paying attention to yourself, your muscles, your motions."

Dr. Panter works the stiff tissue in my shoulder as she delivers her motherly lecture. Not that I don't deserve or need it.

"Laramie, are you hearing me?" I nod at the doctor without seeing her. Her snort proves she isn't buying my bullshit. "You aren't, but I need you to." She pauses in her massage and settles her hands on my shoulders.

Not meeting her eyes, I pick at the sheet draped over the table. A hundred excuses rise and die on my tongue. I want to shrug off her gentle reprimand. Defend. Deny.

"It might be best if you switch to a different time. You're an adult, so I can't force you to do anything, but in my professional opinion, you'll make a faster recovery with better results if you fully focus. And right now..."

She doesn't have to say anything else. I slump forward, huff out a breath, then meet her gaze with mine. "Right now, there are other things diverting my attention."

Her voice is soft and sympathetic. "I'm not suggesting you don't explore your options, but those pursuits are better left outside my office."

"I hear you, Doc. No more eye-banging the other patients." I hope the bravado and humor I inject into my words can conceal the disappointment curling through me. Disappointment with myself, and even sharper, disappointment at the idea of not seeing War again.

Dr. Panter studies me. "You're a smart woman. Sharp. Driven. You'll figure out what you want. If you decide a different time might fit better, stop by the desk before you leave. I'll make sure it happens."

"Thank you." I mean it as I say it. She's right, after all. I need to re-prioritize. I can't let a pretty face derail my dreams.

Five minutes into my soak in the hot tub, the door opens. Lifting my head from the ledge, I see the person I most and least want to. My conversation with Dr. Panter rings in my ears, warning me why I have to get this man out of my head. And along with it, my friendly devils pointing out that now I can move ahead with a roll in the hay. Release my desire and distraction by getting under—or on top of—him. After, I can start fresh in a new time slot and pour my energy into meeting and surpassing my goals.

War cuts an impressive figure, his bright blue swim trunks setting off his golden skin. The water rises as he sinks into the hot tub, his arm casually settling behind me. Like a magpie, my eyes are drawn to the expensive watch still on his wrist. *Must be water resistant.* I wonder if he ever takes it off... The image of War's fingers inside me, the glint of the rose gold cage of his watch glittering between my legs, sends a charge straight to my pussy.

"We have to stop meeting like this, Trouble. At least you weren't underwater this time."

Shifting and covering my brain-haze with a scoff, I say, "I find it interesting how it's always you who follows me in here. A lady might think you have an ulterior motive."

"Oh, no, I'm here for the soothing water, not at all for the beautiful woman." The fine wrinkles around his eyes deepen as he smiles.

"Do you flirt with all the PT patients?" I keep my tone even, but internally I resemble teen me at my first One Direction concert.

"Nope, just you." Everything about him softens as he speaks. "I have a confession." His sexy voice curls around my ears and drips down my spine like honey. I hide a shiver and raise my eyebrows, a silent invitation for him to go on. "I wasn't *just* flirting when I told you I wanted to learn more about you. You're a puzzle I'm desperate to piece together."

Warmth floods my cheeks and down my neck and chest.

Why is that so hot? My tongue tangles, and no words come out.

"I-uh-what?" I finally manage. *Smooth, Laramie.*

War skims a long finger down the exposed portion of my shoulder. "There's something about you, Trouble." My skin tingles where he touches me, and I ache to sink my fingers into his hair.

Swallowing, I lick my lips. "Why were you late today?"

As soon as I ask the question, the spell between us breaks. War straightens, and his hand falls away. Clearing his throat, he says, "I had some family business to take care of. My father and I... we're currently at odds, and since we work together—or did work together..." He trails off before sighing. "It's complicated."

Holy shit. I'm a dumbass. "You're War Phillips, as in Phillips Construction." The wince he makes has me wishing I could suck those words out of existence. He tenses but doesn't say anything else. "Your family bought a horse from my dad. Prairie Sky Equine?"

A flicker of recognition sparks in his eyes. "Crown Dominion."

I nudge him gently, remembering—this time—we both have shoulder injuries. "We just called him Biscuit, but Crown Dominion fits. He's a gorgeous horse."

Some of the tension bleeds from his body, and he shifts enough for our knees to touch. I take the initiative and close the small gap between us, twisting so our bodies press together. Without worrying about the consequences or what may happen, I lean forward and brush my lips against his. "Who knew we had a past?"

Warm air spills from his lips, ghosting over mine. "Another layer of the mystery that is Laramie Larson."

"Not that mysterious. In fact, I'd argue I'm being pretty clear."

War tangles his fingers in my hair, tilting my head where he wants it. The gap between our mouths shrinks. One more millimeter and I'll be able to taste him. We move in slow motion; my stomach clenches and quivers, and my heart pounds like a drum. Can he hear it? Our lips meet, a mere buss. I part my lips, ready for more, as the door to the aquatic therapy room swings open, and we both jerk back, putting a berth of space between us.

The clueless PT patient stares at us for an awkward beat before diving into the hydrotherapy pool on the far side of the room. Our eyes meet, and we break into loud laughter.

Once we gather our wits, silence falls over us. I sink into the water, letting my legs drift toward the surface. Nibbling my lips, I say, "Do you—" as War says, "How did—"

Smiling at him, I wave him on.

"Are you sure?" At my earnest nod, he says, "You grew up around horses; how did you end up riding broncos? Are you an adrenaline junkie?"

"Barrel racing." At the confusion on his face, I shrug. "The bronco was a one-time thing. I'm a barrel racer. And to your other question, that's a piece of it, probably. But I'm not a pain slut, and I don't have a death wish—"

"Hold on. A pain slut?"

This time, my cheeks burn from embarrassment, and I crane my head, thankful when the other patient continues swimming laps, paying us no attention. I can't believe I blurted out *pain slut*. Ducking my head and wiggling my arms in the warm water, I say, "Yeah, you know, the ones who get off on getting hurt. It fills something in them. Let's them feel something. I've seen cowboys cream their jeans when they land face-first in the dirt or take a hoof to the back."

War's eyebrows rise, and his jaw drops. "Cream their jeans?"

The giggle slips from me unbidden. I don't giggle. Laugh, chortle, obnoxiously snort? Sure. But giggle? What is this man doing to me?

Grinning at him, I say, "It's interesting that cream their jeans is all you took from what I said. But what can I say? Rodeo is a harsh mistress."

"Apparently." He appraises me, and I can't tell if I made the puzzle picture clearer or muddied the waters.

"What about you? No offense, but you don't strike me as the thrill-chasing type."

"No, usually I'm not, but recently..." When he pauses, I can't stop myself from soothing the crinkles in his brow away.

"You can't leave me hanging like that."

He flashes a charming grin, but it dims before taking hold. "Maybe another time."

Once again, the momentum between us comes to a screeching halt. I have to fix it, to get my fix of him. Before I know what I'm doing, words tumble from my mouth. "Have dinner with me."

War cocks his head, his brown eyes appraising and curious. "Are you asking me out, Laramie?"

May as well go whole hog. "Yep."

His toothy smile is worthy of a dental billboard. "I'd love to. Can I get your number? Does Friday night work for you?"

I clear my throat. "Tonight. Now."

"Now?" If his eyebrows rise any higher, they'll disappear into his hairline.

My stomach flutters. He probably thinks I'm desperate, and he's not wrong. If I don't do this now, I won't see him again to make it happen. And while I would regret not giving PT my all, I also know I'll forever regret not properly kissing this man.

"Yep. Come on, Pretty Boy. Where's your sense of adventure?"

He rubs his jaw. "It'll be hard to get a decent reservation this late."

"*Pfft*," I make a sound akin to a deflating balloon. "I have the perfect place in mind; no reservation needed."

"You're something else, you know that?"

"So I've been told."

War gets out of the hot tub and helps me out. He wraps a towel around me, his large hands rubbing up and down my arms. Even through the thick material, his touch is a brand searing my skin.

Yes, this is what I need. One night with this intriguing man. One night to burn off this attraction. Then I can focus. Then I can heal.

CHAPTER SIX

war

Outwardly, I'm all cool confidence as I wrap a towel around Laramie. Internally, though, there's a loud, blaring voice that sounds similar to my father screaming, *"What are you doing? This isn't you."* I grit my teeth, fighting to dislodge his disapproving words.

I took a stand today, a stand last week. My life isn't a spiraling mess. Today is the first step in making my future what I want it to be, and what I want right now is to go out with this woman.

This woman I just met. This woman who asked *me* out. On a date I agreed to with no planning. No groundwork. No suit. *Shit.*

"Having second thoughts?" I release the slowly tightening grip I have on her arms. "Did I freak you out? You can say no."

"No!" I startle us both with my yell. Taking a deep breath, I regroup. "No. I want to go out with you, Trouble, but I only have my gym clothes."

Her chocolate brown eyes study me, raking me over from

head to toe. "I have an idea for that, but you'll have to trust me. Give up some of that control you seem to cling to."

"What makes you think I'm controlling?"

"People and horses aren't all that different." Her head slants as she continues to scrutinize me. "You learn to read them. The way they carry themselves, the subtle movements and—" She smiles. "Let's say... quirks that give them away."

"And what did I give away?" I'm genuinely curious. She's not wrong. Everything in my life has been so carefully orchestrated since I was born that I cling to the control I do have. Things like my apartment, my car, my clothing. In bed. I'm also controlling at work, double and triple-checking every document that comes across my desk. Holding tight to the company's social media.

Or at least I did. I guess that's all gone now.

Laramie's sweet drawl calls me back. "There's the way you frown at Dr. Panter when she corrects your form during an exercise. The way your eye is still ticking over my suggestion we go out today." She grasps my wrist, looking at the watch face. "The way you fiddle with that ridiculously expensive watch as if knowing the time, date, and what's probably the planet's current orbital location can give you control."

Damn, she's got a read on me. I can't decide if I like that or find it unnerving. Laramie's thumb caresses my cheek. "Hey, Pretty Boy, there's nothing wrong with needing or wanting control." She leans in so her lips graze mine. "But there's also nothing wrong with letting go."

I step closer, touching as much of her as I can without outright groping her in the aquatic therapy room. My mouth chases hers as she takes a half-step.

"So what's it going to be? In or out?" Her teasing tone and the smirk on her full lips have me in her thrall.

Swallowing, I answer. "In." *All in, Trouble. All in.*

I tug at the fitted jeans Laramie coaxed me into at some discount big-box store before climbing into her truck. This is so far out of my comfort zone I may as well be on another planet. She asked me out. She's driving. She picked my clothes. She paid for them.

Pursing my lips, I mutter, "I look dumb."

"Stop grumbling! You look sexy." Her appreciative gaze rakes over me. "I bet I could bounce a dime off your ass. And don't get me started on your thighs." She waggles her eyebrows. This woman. She is definitely like no one else I've met.

Running my sweaty palms over the denim, I ask, "Where are you taking me that this..." I gesture to the pearl-snap shirt and jeans. "...is an appropriate outfit?"

"Stir-ups."

My brow crinkles in a silent question.

"A fantastic little dive bar that serves the best steak fingers you've ever eaten."

I snort. "The only steak fingers I've ever eaten."

Laramie glances at me as she pulls off the highway and onto a narrow, two-lane road. "Oh, War, you poor, deprived thing. You've really never had a steak finger?"

"Well, we had a cook growing up, and steak fingers weren't exactly on the menu."

"That's a damn shame. I'm happy to help you pop your steak finger cherry."

"The mouth on you."

"You don't know the half of what my mouth can do." She winks before returning her eyes to the road. "Am I too much for you, Pretty Boy? Because this is who I am. Like it or lump it."

I itch to lace my fingers in her hair and kiss her until she's flushed and writhing. The image of Laramie splayed out before me, that sassy mouth commanding me to please her, has me gritting my teeth in a futile attempt at keeping some of my blood above my belt. My voice is rough when I finally answer. "I like it."

I don't miss the way she bites her lower lip or squirms in her seat. My chest swells at her reaction to my words. To me. Laramie is a breath of the freshest air I've ever inhaled.

"So tell me more about you, War. Besides being a former swimmer who injured himself in the water, what do you do?"

I weigh my words. "I worked for my dad at Phillips Construction, which you already know, but recently, I decided to branch out on my own." Not a lie... today is recent, and being disowned means I have no choice but to branch out.

"Really? I figure a family business like that, you'd take the reins from your father in a few years."

"My father and I have different visions, and it was time for me to find where else my strengths lie."

Her eyes cut to me. "My dad owns a stud farm, sir; I know horseshit."

A laugh bubbles up from my chest. "Damn, Trouble, you don't pull any punches, do you?"

"Nope. Want to tell me what you mean behind the corporate double-speak?"

Do I want to tell her? Tell her how I betrayed my sister for years and only just grew brave enough to stick up for her and myself? How I've been railroaded and bullied into a career I didn't want, a life I'd never have chosen for myself?

When I don't answer, her hand drops from the steering wheel and squeezes my thigh. "No pressure. You don't owe me any answers. If you're happy with where you're headed, that's all that matters anyway." She slows the truck as we pull up in front of a building that more closely resembles a shack than any sort of business. "You ready?"

"This is the place?" The bar sits catty-corner to a questionable motel and nothing else. It's as if the two buildings sprang out of the earth in the middle of nowhere. Competing garish neon signs fritz in and out, and the pock-marked parking lot is full of worn gravel and pickups that look like Laramie's.

"Yep."

I consider snapping a selfie in front of this ramshackle bar and sending it to my parents to show them how far I am, physically and emotionally, from the man I've always been. Instead, I nod. "Let's go."

As we enter the smoky, crowded space, I'm thankful for my outfit. I blend in with everyone here. If I'd shown up in a suit, I would have stuck out like a sore thumb. I rest my hand on Laramie's lower back and whisper, "Good call on the clothes, Trouble."

"I've got you."

Those words settle over me, calming my nerves while stoking the embers of my want for her. *She's got me.* In more ways than she even knows. Shaking my head, I try to ignore the unfamiliar feelings powering through me. I don't do fast. Instant connections are for fairy tales and people who deserve them, like Tuesday.

"Hey, Noah, we'll take two house shots, two waters, and two of whatever you've got on tap tonight." Laramie is perfectly at ease, sliding up to the bar. And fucking hot in painted-on boot-cut jeans and a fitted button-up shirt. Her eyes glitter beneath the brim of her cowboy hat, and her long, shiny brown hair cascades down her back in waves. It isn't a look I'm normally drawn to, but on Laramie, it's got me hard as a rock.

"Sure thing, darlin'. You eating too?" I clench my jaw at his overly familiar pet name and press into Laramie's side.

Without missing a beat, she slips her hand into my back pocket as she answers, "Hell, yes. Two specials. We'll be in the corner." Before I can process that she ordered for us, she's leading me across a floor coated with sawdust and peanut shells. Twangy music plays over the speakers, and a handful of people dance off to the side of the bar. Others call out to her in greeting. Laramie waves but doesn't pause on her trek.

When we reach the dimly lit back corner, Laramie tosses her hat onto the table and slides into a curved booth with worn vinyl, patting the seat. When I hesitate, her eyes soften. "You good? I promise I won't bite—unless you're into that."

"Damn, I am so far out of my comfort zone." Despite the boisterous crowd, Laramie hears my mumbled words.

"Hey, if you hate it, we can go. No hard feelings. I get this probably isn't your usual scene."

I huff and settle next to her, hooking my arm around her shoulder. Something about touching her feels so right. "No, it isn't, but maybe that's a good thing. What exactly did you order?"

"The house shots are just the worst, cheapest tequila you've ever tasted served with lime and salt. Tap will be something light and watered down. Tonight's special is the previously promised steak fingers and water..." She grins. "Do I need to explain that one?"

"You're such a smart ass." Without thinking, I drop a kiss to her head and breathe in her subtle and surprisingly floral scent. I freeze, waiting for her reaction, but all Laramie does is snuggle into my chest. Clearing my throat, I say, "The bartender seemed to know you. Are you a regular?"

"Only when I'm in town. I travel a lot during the year, but when I'm at home, I stop here at least once a week."

I'm about to ask her why she travels so much when an older waitress with a tired, kind smile drops a tray on our table. "Hey there, Laramie."

"Hi, Dolores. How's Mel?"

Our waitress—Dolores—snorts and waves a weathered hand. "You know that old SOB. He's as ornery as ever." Dolores leans in and pats Laramie's hand. "We both think it's a real damn shame about your arm. You'd have taken the title this year; I know it."

Laramie's entire body stiffens, her weight shifting slightly as tension pulls her shoulders toward her ears. "There's always next year, right?" Her words are stilted and practiced, and I'm reminded of myself at shareholder meetings promising returns on investments regardless of the state of the economy.

Thanking Dolores, I snag the shots and pass one to Laramie. "How about you show me how this is done, Trouble?"

The relief in her body is instant, and she shifts her attention from Dolores' retreating form back to me. "You've never done a tequila shot? Maybe instead of Pretty Boy, I should call you Sheltered Boy."

A barking laugh rumbles out of me, and I lean into her, dropping to a whisper. "I have done shots before, but you looked like you needed an out. Want to talk about it?"

"Nope, but I do want to lick this salt off you and then suck this lime from your lips."

My mouth drops open, and Laramie takes advantage, sliding the lime between my teeth.

"You okay with this?"

At my nod, my brazen cowgirl snags my arm and rolls up my sleeve. Keeping her eyes locked on mine, she licks the thin skin of my inner wrist. The warm wetness of her tongue has me dropping my head against the warped padding of the booth.

If it feels this good when she licks my wrist, I may not survive having her mouth anywhere else. My mind paints a vivid picture. One of Laramie on her knees, guiding my hands to her head before opening to take me deep. What a way to go.

"Welcome to the afterlife, Warren Phillips. What brings you here?"

"Death by blowjob."

I reach beneath the table and discreetly adjust my cock. If these goddamn pants weren't so tight, I could hide it better. As it stands, anyone within ten feet can see exactly what this woman does to me.

The lime wedge barely stifles my moan when her sweet tongue runs up my skin once more. She drains the shot and leans forward, her lips pressing to mine as she sucks the sliced fruit.

It's over far too quickly. My cock throbs, and I swear I'll let her use my body for all her eating and drinking needs from now on if it means putting her mouth on me again.

"Your turn." Laramie slowly parts her lips, allowing me to slide the lime wedge into her mouth. She offers me her wrist, and I mirror her actions, relishing the taste of her.

My pulse pounds as I lap up each grain of salt, throw back the shot, and capture her mouth, draining the lime dry.

She wasn't lying; this is the cheapest, nastiest tequila I've ever had, and nothing has ever tasted better.

When I break away, her pupils have eaten up the brown of her eyes, leaving them like midnight without a moon. Laramie's hand cups the back of my head and she pulls me in, her fingers grasping the short hair at my nape. The kiss is demanding, hungry, and perfect. There's no gentle exploration.

It's a mutual conquering. Each of us taking and giving, battling and conceding control.

She tastes like lime and the sharp bite of the tequila, and this just became the best date I've ever been on.

It isn't until a gentle cough sounds that we break apart. "You two wanna come up for air? Or at least for food?" Dolores gives us a cheeky smirk.

"You have the worst timing." Laramie laughs, fanning her flushed cheeks as she takes our order from the waitress.

"Oh, to be young and beautiful again. All caught up in those first-date flutters."

"I've seen you and Mel; you two are disgustingly in love."

Dolores blushes. "Alright, enough of that. Can I get you anything else?"

"Three more rounds of shots, please."

Three more? She really might be trying to kill me—or make me come in my pants.

When Dolores drops the drinks off, Laramie crooks a finger. I offer her my wrist, but she shakes her head. Then, with a slow smirk, she says, "Not there." She tilts my head and laps at the side of my neck before sprinkling salt there. This time when she goes to lick my skin, she nips too, then soothes away the sting before downing her shot.

Desire, desperate and hot, courses through me when Laramie cants her head, exposing the slender column of her neck. Like it has a mind of its own, my hand settles around her throat, my thumb skimming over her pulse point. I love the way it paces at my touch. At her shudder, I lean in. Instead of licking, I place an open-mouth kiss on her neck. Followed by a second one. And a third for good measure. Only when she's squirming and making soft, needy sounds do I sprinkle the salt on her skin.

Hours pass in a blur. Talking, laughing, lingering touches. Kisses that almost reach the point of no return. Before I know it, we've downed shots three and four. Who knew steak fingers and cheap tequila pair together so well? Throughout the meal, the salt has found new and unique places to be licked from, and the time spent sucking the juice from the lime has grown.

"I need to share this with Manon, my parents' cook." I fight back a hiccup as I drag a French fry through a mixture of cream gravy and ketchup before feeding it to Laramie, groaning when she nibbles the tips of my fingers.

"Told ya, Pretty Boy. Food of the gods. Or at least of the hungry and tipsy."

When Dolores clears the baskets—not plates—from the table, I slump against the booth, nursing the warm beer Laramie ordered when we first arrived. I clear my throat. "Do you have anything else planned for the evening? If not, I'll call us a car." At her single raised eyebrow, I add, "Separate, of course."

Laramie's hand skates up my thigh as she leans closer. The soft brush of her breath tickles my ear as she whispers, "How about instead of a car, you get us a room? We can sleep off the tequila at The Rusty Spur? Or, even better..." Her teeth scrape my lobe. "Work it off."

Holy shit. Who is this woman, and how can I convince her to be mine?

CHAPTER SEVEN
Laramie

I could drive my truck through War's open mouth.

He straightens, his honey-brown eyes searching mine. "You want to get a room?"

The evening has been hours of foreplay: every kiss, every teasing touch, every heated look. I can see he's as affected as I am, thanks to the fit of the jeans he's wearing.

"Yeah, Pretty Boy. I want to get a room." I skim my nose down his jaw while my hand slides higher up his thigh. "To spend the night with you."

His Adam's apple bobs in his throat. Watching this man swallow is like erotic art. The thought of War on the bed beneath me, moaning as I lick a path over his bare skin, sends desire burning through me.

Until, like a bucket of cold water, I realize he still hasn't answered. A sliver of doubt slithers through me, and I pull away and move my hand from his leg. "Shit. I'm sorry. I thought..." I hold my hands up. "If you're not feeling this or don't want to fu... sleep with me—"

He silences me with his lips. There's depth to this kiss, a

yearning. A shiver slinks from my scalp to my spine as his tongue smoothly strokes mine. I lean into the caress of his hands as they wander from my arms to my shoulders before settling on my back, holding me tight. I'm not misreading the situation. He wants this. Wants me.

War's lips hover over mine as he rasps, "Trust me when I say I've been thinking of how good it would be between us since I laid eyes on you last week."

I nuzzle my face into the crook of his neck and suck on the pulse point there. "If you haven't figured it out, I hate going slow, but be honest. Am I moving too fast?"

"Maybe I need someone to encourage me to pick up the pace." He smirks and lifts my chin. "How about we get out of here?"

"Yeah?"

"Yeah."

I sweep my hat off the table and plop it onto his head. His eyebrows quirk. "Claiming me, Trouble?"

"You know the saying. Wear the hat, and the cowgirl rides you."

He lets out a loud laugh that draws attention from the people around us. "That's not quite how I remember it."

Shrugging, I lay cash on the table to cover our tab and meal, plus a generous tip for Dolores. "Hmm, your memory is slipping in your old age. Come on, let's get out of here."

War frowns at the cash, then me. "Laramie—"

"I asked, so I pay. Plus, this is one more way for you to practice giving up some of that control." Moving closer to him, I add, "Once we get to the room, I have a few more ways you can practice."

His responding growl is a direct line to the warmth building in my stomach. I want to make him pant and moan and keen. For me. To have him on his knees with his groans buried in my pussy. For my noises of satisfaction to come from around the thick length of his cock.

My heart thrums, the rhythm echoed by the throbbing between my thighs. I lace our fingers together and drag him out the door. The crisp December air does little to cool the fire scorching my blood. In an instant, I'm on War. Lust riding me hard.

He's used to leading, but I give as good as I get, running my tongue over his teeth, nibbling and sucking his bottom lip into my mouth.

"Fuck, Laramie," War pants.

"Yes. That's the idea." I tug on his hand again as we stumble across the gravel parking lot toward The Rusty Spur. The ancient neon sign flickers, half the letters burned out so only *h usy pur* remain.

"Welcome to the *Hussy Purr*, Pretty Boy." *Shit, maybe I should have stopped at three shots tonight.* No, it isn't tequila I'm drunk on; it's War Phillips.

I fight off a snort of glee at the shock and disgust on War's face. He blinks, then blinks again as if this will change the questionable exterior of the motel into five-star accommodations.

"This is where you want to stay?"

Elbowing him, I tease, "Don't be a snob!"

He squints and waves at the dingy building, where the night clerk is visible behind the plexiglass of his office. "It's not about being a snob. I-it's about standard health regulations. This is how people get bed bugs."

I nudge him, mindful of our shoulders. "Come on, where's your sense of adventure? I have a spare turnout blanket in my truck."

"Trouble, you are living up to every inch of your name."

My smile pulls at my cheeks, impossible to hold back. "Did I steer you wrong on the steak fingers?"

"No, but—"

"Then trust me. I promise to ask for the nicest room they have." Chucking his chin, I add, "I'll even let you pay."

War crosses his arms, but when he sighs and rolls his eyes, I know I have him.

Sliding up to the window, I rap against the glass. "Hey, Mel, we need your best room."

"Mel? As in Dolores and Mel?" War glances between the bar and the motel.

"One and the same."

Mel ambles toward us and slides the small partition open, his wizened face lighting up at the sight of us. "Laramie! Good to see ya, girly. Did you say hi to Dolly? She'll have my hide if you came here without stopping in."

"Don't worry; you're in the clear. We had dinner first. Can we get a room? My date's getting cold."

Mel looks over at War and winks. "Nice hat."

War's hand flies to my Stetson, still resting on his head, and pink colors his cheeks.

"No reason to be embarrassed, young man. How do you think Dolly and I started out?" Mel lets out a raspy laugh.

With a grumble, War hands over his credit card and gets the old-fashioned metal key, complete with a palm-sized plastic keychain attached.

"Room 101. You two enjoy!"

"Don't worry, Mel, we will," I shout as War pulls me away and laughter overtakes me.

"You think you're funny, don't you?" War mutters. As we reach the door, his arm bands around my waist, and he twirls me so my back meets the faux-stucco wall outside our room. The key clatters to the ground, and his fingers weave into my hair, guiding my head where he wants me. From beneath the wide brim of my hat, he kisses me. Lips firm and punishing, not bothering to wait for my answer. A ragged moan spills from my throat when his thigh slips between my knees. Waves of pleasure crash over me, and I drop my head back, not minding the bite of pain where it hits with a thud.

I ache to guide *him* exactly where I want him most. For now, I settle for rocking against his leg, searching out that wonderful friction. Like I'm a puppet, he pulls my strings, maneuvering my hips, marshaling my pace. It's not quite enough. While the coarse seam of my jeans hits just right, I need more. Faster. Harder. A slightly different angle. I squirm and roll in desperate circles.

I'm so close.

Heat pools at the base of my spine and spreads, raising prickles along my skin. That glorious edge is in sight.

Ready to fall.

Ready to expl—

"Not yet, Trouble."

I groan when I lose purchase on War's leg—and my orgasm. Jutting my lip out, I reach for his hand, but he spins me and presses his front to my back. The length of his cock twitches against me, so I do what comes naturally and press back.

"Shit. You are going to kill me." He pins my ass against his hips and thrusts once. "You've been running this date all night, teasing me about giving up control, but it's time you gave up some instead." Leaving one hand digging into my waist, the other fists my hair, tugging it to the side before his mouth travels the length of my neck, leaving a burning trail of love bites.

For a heartbeat, we're apart as he snags the discarded key, fumbling it against the lock until it clicks open. Together, we crash through the door into a heap of arms, legs, teeth, tongues, and longing.

It's a mad dash—a flurry of buttons and *zips*. A race to see who can undress the other faster, as if the winner will retain control over the other's pleasure. Ultimately, no matter how this plays out, we'll both be winners.

I strip away his pearl snap shirt, snap his belt from the loops, and tug off his jeans until War is left in only his tight, black boxer briefs.

He's exquisite.

I soak in the masculine lines of his lean but well-muscled body. The veins in his forearms, where he still wears the fancy timepiece. The smattering of reddish-brown hair that dapples his chest, tapers off, and then reappears, darker and thicker, below his navel. The ridges of his stomach and... I lick my lips, every atom of my being hyper-focused on the way his cock strains against his boxer briefs, a deliciously thick treat begging to be tasted.

When I finally tear my eyes away, I find him appreciating me in the same way. The heat of his stare is like a beam piercing through me. Can he see my failures? My ambition? How much I want him? How much I wish I'd met him in another life so I could keep him? I shift my weight, reminding myself of who I am and why I'm here, before taking a breath, tossing my hair, and arching my back.

The bright red panties with black cats all over them and the non-matching sheer orange bra aren't landing me a lingerie ad anytime soon, but War doesn't seem to mind. Especially when I toss the bra at his head.

It's as if we're in a high-noon showdown, each of us standing and staring. Silently demanding the other to take the next step.

Giving an inch, War licks his lips with the grin of a man

confident in what he's bringing to the table, tugs his boxer briefs down, and frees his cock from the confines of its cotton prison.

It's a gorgeous cock, just like its owner. War strides toward me, wearing nothing but his watch and a smile as he strokes the thick, veiny length. He moves forward until his chest is against mine, leaving the hot heat of him pinned between us. The faint sensation of dampness trails on my stomach. The overwhelming need to touch him, taste him, feel him has me reaching between our bodies. I glide my hand over his cock, scarcely touching him, before flirting with the type of pressure that will make him fall apart.

"Such a tease." He croaks the words and tips his head before snapping his greedy gaze to my tits. His long fingers skate over my sides, then higher, until they stop to trace slow circles around my pebbled nipples. "So beautiful."

Reaching around him, I snag my discarded hat. With a coy pout, I say, "You're too tall for me to put it on you from there." We both know it isn't true, but I want to see what he'll do. If he'll concede control once more.

My blood turns to molten honey, and my hat falls from my hands—completely forgotten—when he sinks to his knees. Petal-soft kisses flutter over my sternum and stomach, brushing my hips and the sides of my thighs. Then he buries his nose into the lacy material of my panties.

"You want to take these off?"

Gripping his hair, I tilt his head, guiding him to look up at me. "I want you to."

"Fuck. Trouble, you've already got me kneeling." But he hooks his fingers in the elastic of my panties and tugs them down my legs. When they pool at my feet, I widen my stance, giving him a better view of, well, everything.

"Now what?" I swear I can feel the tension in his whispered words.

"Now, I want you to be a good boy and make me come."

Whatever thread of control was balancing between us snaps, and War wraps his arms around my thighs and rushes to stand. He takes two tottering steps before dropping me onto the mattress, the springs creaking beneath our weight. Then, like I'm water at the end of a twelve-hour workday in one hundred-degree temps, his mouth is on me.

A pained groan rumbles against my clit. "*Laramie.*"

The way he moans my name sends a fresh wave of arousal to my core, and I must be flooding his mouth. War pants against me, the warmth sending waves of desire crashing over me. He sucks my lower lips, then thrusts his tongue into me, mimicking the rhythm of his hips against the mattress.

It's a whirl of sensations: hot licks, grazing teeth, soothing kisses. Then he slips a single finger into my pussy. One quickly becomes two, and when he curls his fingers, pressing against the magical spot inside me, I let my baser instincts take over.

My walls contract around his fingers, and he lets out another needy moan. "I'll be your good boy, Trouble," he promises against my pussy. "But only if you come all over my face."

The warring sensations of his talented tongue tracing figure-eights around my clit and his nimble fingers combating for supremacy inside me push me to the brink. A delicious jolt surges through my body, and I cry out as I come, stars bursting behind my eyes.

War gentles two more kisses to my clit, then nuzzles his lips and messy chin against my inner thigh. "You're the best thing I've ever tasted."

I fling an arm over my eyes and smile into the crook of my

elbow. "Even better than the steak fingers and tequila?" I bask in his responding laugh like it's the sun.

"Yeah, sweetheart, way better."

My stomach flutters at the sincerity in his words, along with a heaping dose of guilt. Am I really going to walk out on this man?

On one side, I have Dr. Panter's advice about focusing while I'm in PT. My goals. My plans. On the other is a connection I never expected. Turmoil coils through me like a snake slithering for shelter.

But then War rests his head on my stomach and trails a hand up my side, banishing all those worries and leaving lust and a much deeper longing behind.

Embracing the emotions, I lift War's face and swoop my lips over his before sneaking my tongue between them. With a soft nip, I say, "I promised to ride you, Pretty Boy, and that's what I'm gonna do."

He grunts when I give him a playful shove so I can climb off the bed and find my jeans. Snagging the slim pack of condoms from my pocket, I saunter back to him. "You ready for this?"

A dark growl rumbles from his throat, and he scrambles to lie on the bed. As soon as he's settled, I'm astride him, legs spread wide over his hips. He's so sexy, his hair rumpled, his pupils dilated, his cheeks flushed.

I stroke his cock, my thumb swiping the bead of pre-cum at his crown, bringing it to my mouth. With a whimper, I suck his flavor from my skin. "Are you ready?" I repeat. What I mean is, are you sure? Do you really want me?

He nods, digging his fingers into my hips.

"Say it. I want to hear you."

"I'm so fucking ready, Laramie. And so are you. You're dripping for me."

I yank open the condom and roll it down his length. Then,

with a teasing grin, I rub my pussy against the flared head of his cock, not taking him in. Not yet. Instead, I tease us both, lowering myself so that just the tip broaches my slit before rising up and away.

"Trouble," War grits out from clenched teeth.

"Tell me what you want."

"You know what I want."

I repeat my movements, rising and dropping just enough to take the first half inch of him into my core before pulling away. "No, be specific. Tell me *exactly* what you want."

He grunts and swallows. "Fuck. I want you to ride me until I come inside your perfect pussy. Is that what you want to hear?"

"Good boy." I reward him by sinking down, taking him inch by inch, loving the *fucks* and *shit, sweethearts* spilling from his lips. Why are man moans so damn sexy?

I give myself a minute to adjust, enjoying the heat of his hard cock inside me. His thumbs press into my hips, and he grits as if fighting the longing to chase what he needs.

"So good. So patient, waiting for me to tell you to move," I croon at him as I work myself up and down his length in slow, sensuous strokes. Leaning back against his raised knees, I purr, "Look at us, Pretty Boy. We're a perfect fit."

His honey eyes snap to where we meet, and at the plea in his wordless groan, I rotate my hips. And he lets out a wanton groan when I shift so my clit slides against the lowest part of his stomach over and over again. The world-warping sensation of him inside me, the pressure where I need it most, his scent, the twitch of his muscles—god, it's glorious. I grip his shoulders, my fingers digging in like he's all that's tethering me to reality.

With each writhing circle I make, he thrusts up, watching me from below like I'm something special. Something he can't live without. A primal urge comes over me, and I lean forward, capturing his lips with my own. Usually I'm not much for this level of intimacy during sex, but I can't get enough of this man's drugging kisses. Our tongues tangle and twist, another point of connection between us.

Chest to chest, mouth to mouth, locked together in the most ancient of ways.

My thighs burn as I grind and rock against him, chasing my climax and his. Each glorious press of his hard pelvis against my clit brings me closer to the edge. But I'm not going alone.

"Do it, War. Come."

"Not until you do." His hands glide along my skin, roaming from my hips, up my sides, and then down to grab my ass, spreading me wide.

"You feel so fucking good." He mutters the praise against my mouth, his breath slipping into my lungs.

So does he. Full and thick and strong and warm. I clench my innermost muscles, wanting to bring War along with me. Not daring to leave him behind, not on this.

"Yes, just like that, Trouble. Squeeze me." War thrusts deep, and my muscles tense, my body simultaneously trying to pull him in and push him out.

"War!" His name is a battle cry, a triumph, an exaltation. Just as it's been for centuries before, only this time, I'm the one conquered.

As if triggered by my orgasm, my Pretty Boy comes, the heat of his release tangible even through the thin latex of the condom. We collapse into a spent heap, his softening cock still inside me.

"*Where it belongs,*" one of my devils whispers. The other remains oddly silent.

War wraps his arms around me, my head cradled in the

nook of his neck. Our chests rise and fall in unison as we work to come down from the high of our shared release.

"That was..." I trail off, not sure how to finish the sentence. How can it be like this? How can any one person make me feel so alight? So alive? So right?

Fingers comb through my hair and run over my body as if checking me for injury. Then, with a touch so careful, you'd think I was porcelain, War kisses me. This kiss, more than any other tonight, shakes something in me. It's the one where I become irreversibly addicted to this man and break both our hearts.

Thankfully, War rises with a groan before I can dig further into those thoughts. He pinches off the used condom, knots it, and then tosses it into the nearby trash can. When he tugs on his boxer briefs and steps into the small bathroom, I wonder if he'll be the one to suggest we part ways—making this easier on me.

Instead, he returns with a damp washcloth. A pang of affection warms me. This part of sex is one I'm less familiar with. I'm usually here for the flash. The bang. Not the cuddle and the cleanup.

While War tenderly wipes away the mess, I study the popcorn ceiling above our heads, gnawing my lower lip like it's a bit. Unease and guilt knot in my stomach. This man doesn't deserve a *love 'em and leave 'em* moment. And certainly not one at The Rusty Spur.

What is he doing here with me? He should be drinking wine in Uptown with a leggy blonde who has soft hands and perfect nails. A woman who would concede to his dominance and be there for him in the morning. Not a speed-chasing cowgirl who doesn't have room in her life for anything but getting better.

I'm so lost in my thoughts that I miss him climbing into

bed. It isn't until his arms wrap around me and he presses his lips to my neck that it registers. He's talking to me.

"Sorry, what?"

He chuckles. "What did Dolores mean when she said you'd have taken the title?"

Great. The one thing I *don't* want to talk about. I clear my throat. "You caught that, huh?"

"I caught you tensing up in my arms and heard words that sound like you practice them in front of a mirror slipping out."

He's too good for me. I'm an asshole. I swallow and say, "I told you I'm a barrel racer." At his nod, I continue. "This week is the national finals. I, um, should be there competing right now."

War tugs on my shoulder, his brow creasing as he hovers over me. "So you do that full-time? Like a job? I guess I thought it was a hobby or something."

"Definitely not a hobby."

My terse answer doesn't derail the conversation. "I didn't know that... is that why you travel so much, too?"

Dipping my head, I say, "Gotta go where the purses and the points are."

"Traveling like that must make relationships hard."

"Why do you say that?" There's a sharpness to my question and to my fingers digging into the bed.

My tone catches him off guard. "Well, I mean anyone who travels that much, unless you're good with long distances, it would strain—I'm guessing. Do you usually date—"

I cut his stammer off with my mouth.

Kissing War is effortless, but pushing down the storm of growing feelings for him isn't. But tonight has to be it. He's a distraction—a beautiful distraction. I would love to see where this could go, but I can't afford it.

Refocusing on the delicious man above me, I nip his full

bottom lip and tug. His hips pin me to the bed, pressing into me in a slow, seductive grind. Each movement causes whimpers to escape my mouth. With an aching moan, War breaks the kiss and shifts his weight, pulling me into his arms and resting his chin on the crown of my head.

"If refractory periods weren't a real thing, I'd take you again right now."

I tilt my head back and laugh, thankful for the change in topic. "Let me get us some water." As I move, I poke his thigh with my toe. "To help with your recovery."

War props himself up against the headboard, watching me pad across the room to get a plastic cup. With one arm behind his head, he looks for all the world like the snack of my dreams. We pass the tepid tap water back and forth until it's gone, and then I slip beneath the sheets.

I rest my chin on his chest and drink in my fill of him like the greedy goblin I am.

"Agreeing to go on this date and ending up in bed with you are probably in the top five most impulsive things I've ever done."

"You never packed up and took a road trip somewhere new or got a dealer's choice tattoo? Not even when you were..." I smirk. "Young?"

With a mutter, War rolls us and pins me to the bed. "Again with the old thing? I'm six years older than you, not sixty."

My laugh is breathy as I stare up at him. "You'll just have to prove how virile you are, Pretty Boy."

"That's an oxymoron, you know? Calling me Pretty *Boy* and an old man all at once."

"You're an oxymoron. Now kiss me and then answer my original question. You've never done anything reckless or irresponsible?"

Following my command, he sinks his mouth against mine.

The plush give of his lips sends a fresh wave of arousal through me. War tastes like the remnants of the drinks we shared and the lingering flavor of my orgasm. It's heady and delicious—my new favorite.

A hum escapes my lips when he coils a tangled strand of my hair around his finger. "No. Never. I was always the yes man, the perfect son. Anything that would make my parents look bad or damage the company's reputation was never on the table."

"Sounds boring. And stifling. You're supposed to be impulsive and make mistakes when you're young. And your parents should be there to teach you why you shouldn't steal the tractor and chase the neighbor's stud bull."

He huffs a laugh into my hair. His words have a bitter edge. "You and I had very different childhoods."

Using every ounce of strength in my thighs, I twist until I'm straddling his torso. Then I wriggle until my pussy rests against the base of his cock. He grows thicker and firmer with each glide of my wet center against him until he's at full attention. I grip the base of his cock, pumping him from tip to root, then rubbing his hard length against my clit and between my lower lips.

"God, you look like some sort of queen sitting there." I love how his hips buck as if he has no control over them. As if he can't keep himself from chasing that connection—fullness for me and tight heat for him.

"Do you want to talk more about what happened today? Or those other top five impulsive moments?" I ask, writhing against the base of his cock.

War's hands rise to my hips, squeezing as I rock against him. "The rest of my list is tied to today. But honestly, you don't seem like you want to talk anymore."

I stroke his cheek, and in the flickering glow of the neon

signs outside our window, I drink him in. Softening my voice, I say, "I'm a pretty good listener, War. I also happen to be a wonderful distraction. The question is, which do you need more?"

Crunching up, he snags my lips with his. "Talk later. Distraction now."

Blackness seeps into the room. The creeping dark that precedes the dawn. *This is it, Laramie. You should go. You've stayed too long as it is.*

I blink back the burning in my eyes. I don't want to go. I want to stay. Here. In Mel and Dolores' crappy little motel. In a too-small bed. With a man I hardly know but long to.

War is out cold beside me, his soft breathing an arresting contrast to his hard body. The warm weight of his arm around my waist is an anchor, but it isn't drowning me. No, it's simply mooring me. Keeping me steady.

But steady has never been my goal. And War, with his business suits and fancy Dallas life, doesn't fit into the foolhardy future I'm chasing.

Swallowing the lump in my throat, I carefully lift his arm. Once I'm out of his hold, I take one last look. One last chance to capture him in my memories. Placing a kiss on his forehead, I whisper, "I'm sorry."

Then, I run.

CHAPTER EIGHT

war

Trail Creek, New Mexico
March

I plop down next to my sister, where she sits with Bond—her fiancé—his sister Charli, and their friends, Griff and Dane. I'm not exactly feeling social, but meeting up at The Bee and The Bean, the local bakery and coffee shop Bond's other sister, Clairy, owns has become part of my new normal.

With bloodshot and bleary eyes, I study my pecan coffee as if the delicious dark roast can give me the answers I'm searching for. My phone vibrates in my pocket again. I already know who it is—and who it isn't—and it's no one I want to talk to.

"War?" My name registers, but only barely. "Earth to War!" This time, Tuesday snaps, her voice cutting through last night's bourbon fog.

I grin despite her scolding. I love that she's growing comfortable enough to yell at me. "Sorry, what?"

"Have you thought any more about Bond's offer to come on

permanently at Davis Designs?" The man in question kisses the top of her head.

The bell above the door tinkles as another patron enters the busy shop. "No." I drain my coffee, hoping the caffeine will kick in sooner if I drink it fast enough.

"Care to elaborate?" She gives me an expectant look.

Shrugging, I say, "I'm enjoying the day-to-day work, and I appreciate you offering, but construction isn't my future."

"Davis Designs isn't Phillips Construction." She says it gently, as if mentioning our father's company will send me into a spiral. The single buzz of an incoming text is the more likely culprit of any potential meltdowns, though.

I slide the phone out and glance at the lock screen.

> **WARREN PHILLIPS**
> It's been three months. You made your point. Now stop being a disappointment and…

The message preview cuts off there, but it's more of the same. Another not-so-subtle demand I return to Dallas. Return to my *rightful* place at PC.

Clenching my hands around my mug, I mutter, "Fuck that."

Every head at the table swivels, staring me down.

"Shit, I, uh, I mean, I know." Sighing, I lower my shoulders away from my ears and loosen my jaw. Tuesday doesn't know about the constant calls or messages.

Because you're keeping it from her. The annoyingly perceptive voice is right. I am keeping it from her. Not telling her is easy to justify with the rapid escalation of contact. Tuesday is happy here. The last thing she needs is to hear how Mommy and Daddy Dearest are attempting to stack the blame for my dissension on her.

Giving her hand a quick squeeze, I clear my throat. "The

entire Davis Designs business model is the antithesis of every tenet Warren Phillips ever held. Not only do you care about your employees and customers, but your focus is on building beautiful homes, not soulless skyscrapers." *Or anything that will make you money regardless of the cost.*

"Then what's the problem? You've made friends here, and we..."

I swallow the lump in my throat at her unsaid words. We've made so many strides forward in our relationship. I've learned more about my sister in the past twelve weeks than I had in the prior lifetime of being her twin.

"Anyone need a refill?" I ask, looking for an excuse to step away. I stalk to the glass counter and snag the coffee pot from Clairy, taking my time topping off everyone's drinks.

Why don't I want to stay here and buy into the business Tuesday and Bond are growing? There are tons of reasons. I don't want to encroach on the life she's built. I don't want to be in construction.

It's certainly not because I'm holding out hope that a chestnut-haired cowgirl will ride into town, begging me to run away with her. Nope. Not hung up on the woman who ghosted me after one amazing night at all.

I don't realize my palm is rubbing over the sting in my chest until a small hand lights on the crook of my elbow. "You can talk to me, War." I meet eyes that mirror my own. "You seem so, I don't know... adrift, maybe?"

"I'm exploring my options." I try for a cavalier smirk, but I can tell from her reaction it comes out as a grimace.

"Promise you'll consider it, okay? We'd love to have you stay. The whole town would. Everyone adores you, even with the depression beard."

I scrub a hand over my thick facial hair while Tuesday tuts.

"Seriously, if your goal is to go back to Dallas incognito, you nailed it," Bond calls from our table.

I match Bond's teasing tone. "First, I'm not going back to Dallas. Second," I continue, gesturing to where Griff sits, eating a sea salt croissant, "a lot of the guys around here have beards."

Tuesday's nose wrinkles. "Yeah, well, the Viking can pull it off; you look like a yeti."

"Damn, sis, how do you really feel?" I turn to her friends. "Clairy, Charli, be honest. Is it that bad?"

Clairy laughs. "I like it. It's very mountain man chic."

Charli thinks before she gives her diplomatic answer. "It's definitely different from the way you looked when you showed up in Trail Creek, but it's growing on me."

Tuesday sighs. "Fine, leave it, but at least put some beard oil on it or trim it or something."

I catch my distorted reflection in The Bee and The Bean's window. My flannel shirt is unbuttoned over a plain, fitted white T-shirt, half tucked into a pair of worn jeans. My shaggy hair and shaggier beard conceal a portion of my face. The watch on my wrist is the only part of me that resembles the War of old.

The past few months have been... challenging. When I woke up that December morning to an empty bed, no Laramie in sight, I understood what rock bottom felt like: unemployed, estranged from my parents, needing to reconcile with my sister, and left in a cold motel with the faint memory of a whispered *"I'm sorry."*

There was nothing left for me in Dallas.

In a move that would have made Laramie proud—while climbing to the top of my impulsive behavior list—I packed up my high-rise condo, sold it and most of my belongings, and hit the road.

Despite the distance between us, my sister opened her home and arms to me without question—proving again how wrong I was for the way I treated her all those years. She and her circle of friends, the family she built around herself when my parents—and I—forced her out of Dallas, have welcomed me as if I belong.

Guilt swarms my gut, souring the coffee that sits there. Another reason I can't join Davis Designs? I *don't* belong here. I'm a single dark cloud in an otherwise clear sky. A reminder of the life Tuesday left behind and the pain that went with it.

"I'm heading out. I was supposed to be at one of the new sites ten minutes ago," I say, ignoring the protest that chimes around the table as I wave goodbye. The fresh mountain air slips into my lungs when I step out of the cafe, and the sun catches on the face of my watch. I frown at the timepiece, one of the few things from Dallas I couldn't part with.

The bespoke suits, the hand-crafted Italian shoes, all the trappings of my old life—I packed them away, hiding them in the closet of the small A-frame style cabin I'm renting here in Trail Creek, everything but the watch. The Breitling was an extravagant gift from my father on my 30th birthday, but the damn thing feels like a part of me. So even though it's a marker of my former life and doesn't match my mood or clothing, I wear it daily.

Laramie's assertion that I fiddled with it when I felt out of control plays in my mind, triggering memories of that night—and me wearing nothing but the watch as I made her come. "Fucking hell, War, it's been three months. You've got to get over her." I curse myself, stomping to the Bronco I purchased after selling off my sleek sports car.

Once I'm behind the wheel, my phone automatically connects to the Bluetooth, and as if it knows, it rings. I don't know why I do it, but for the first time in twelve weeks, I hit answer on my father's call and brace myself for his condescension and anger.

"War? It's about time you answered my call. I've been trying to reach you for months."

"I noticed."

"And you thought that was appropriate? To ignore me? To abandon your responsibilities? I expect this sort of behavior from Tuesday, but not you." When I don't respond, he blows out a long breath. "I'm, um, I'm sorry."

If my truck were moving, I probably would've driven into a ditch at his half-hearted apology. "What?"

"I made a..." He pauses as if whatever he has to say is caught in his throat. "A mistake. I'd like to see you. To meet in person. For the two of us to talk things over. See if we can't figure something out." His voice breaks, and for a fraction of a second, I almost believe he means it.

"Figure what out? You told me you'd disown me over helping my sister after you tried to push her into a marriage with the man who released pictures of her without her consent. You backed him over your daughter."

"So did you at first," he snaps, sounding much more like the Warren Phillips I know.

"Yes, and I was wrong. So fucking wrong."

"I'm not going to be around forever. Phillips Construction is your future. It was always meant to be yours."

I sidestep the guilt trip. "If I remember correctly, you said there was nothing that said the company had to stay in the family."

My father clears his throat, and I can picture him in his ostentatious study, fingers drumming on his expensive desk, my mother fluttering around him, eavesdropping. "It was the heat of the moment."

My mother's muffled words come through the line. "Ask him again, Warren."

"Your mother and I feel it would be best for us to talk in person. I'm sure you don't want to come to Dallas, and I won't be coming there."

The scoff is out of my mouth before I can stifle it. "No, I can't imagine you would."

There's a brief shuffle, and then my mom's voice rings over the speaker. "War, baby, please. Meet your dad in Lubbock. It's halfway between you. Neutral. The two of you can talk things over, and we can move forward and put this whole ugly... situation behind us."

"A conversation isn't going to solve anything."

"Don't say that! We're a family," Mom pushes. When the silence stretches between us, she can't help but add, "Do you know how embarrassing this is for us?"

And there it is.

"So none of this is actually about Tuesday or me. It's about you. Like always. Let me guess: the shareholders want to know why both of your children left the company? And your friends at the club are asking why they didn't see us over the holidays?"

When neither of my parents answer, I know I've hit the nail on the head. My bitter laugh sounds in the quiet of my car. "So, thanks for the call. It's been great chatting, but I have to get to work."

"Warren!" The desperation in how my father says my name keeps me from ending the call, but I don't answer him. He quickly fills in the silence between us. "Dinner. A drink. Lubbock, four days from now. Just give me a chance to talk things through."

The tightness in my chest that eased over the past few months comes roaring back, gripping my lungs like a vise.

The first thrums of a headache pound in my temple, but I don't hang up. In a stranger's voice, I say, "Drinks. That's all."

And I hate myself for it.

TUESDAY

Hey, where are you? The crew is going to The Great Dane for karaoke and Flocked Up Flamingos

I'm in Lubbock

???

Why on earth are you in Lubbock?

I scrub a hand through my messy hair. It hangs limp, almost covering my eyes. Shoving it out of my face, I replay the many practice conversations I had with myself preparing for this. None of them are good enough.

I'm sorry. I'm meeting Dad.

...

The dots bounce and disappear until I can't take it anymore.

It's not what you think. I promise. He begged me to hear him out. I'm here for one drink to see what he has to say. That's all.

...

Again, the bouncing dots taunt me.

> Tuesday, please, don't hate me.

I don't hate you, War. Just be careful.

I suck in a ragged breath and type words I've only said to her a handful of times.

> I will. Love you.

I tuck my phone away when she doesn't reply. No sense in adding to my already strained nerves. This evening has all the makings of a gigantic clusterfuck. I should have told her about this before I left Trail Creek.

When I got into town about an hour ago, I drove to the bar where we agreed to meet. I picked one I knew he'd hate. It reminds me of Stir-ups—a ramshackle building with blue-collar clientele. Several TVs behind the bar play clips from a rodeo. The woman on a horse running at a dead sprint around metal barrels snags my attention.

When the bartender sets a second bourbon in front of me, I incline my head toward the screen. "Hey, is that live?"

"Yeah, it's night one of the High Plains Stampede."

It's on the tip of my tongue to ask for more information, but then a throat clears behind me.

Turning on the barstool, I come face to face with my father for the first time since early December. He's aged in the time apart. Three months looks like ten years. He has bags under his eyes, and his pristine hair is far more salt than pepper. His suit is wrinkled, and his tie is loose around his neck. But there's not a part of me that feels sorry for him. Maybe that makes me a bad son, but my loyalty to Tuesday outweighs any regret I have about the state of my *relationship* with my father.

I catch him studying me in much the same way. I'm sure my appearance is as much of a shock to him. My rumpled, practical clothing, my unkempt hair and beard. The extra pounds I've put on.

"Son."

"Father."

After that warm greeting, our stare-off continues. Neither of us speaks, waiting for the other to move first. Like predators watching prey.

He breaks first. *War, one.* "Shall we find somewhere to talk?" He eyes the bar with disdain.

Grunting in reply, I drain my glass and signal the bartender for two more. Once I have the drinks, I lead Warren Phillips to a small booth.

"So, you wanted to meet. Why?" I ask as I shove a bourbon toward him.

"Straight to the point. I can respect that." He takes a long draw of the cheap alcohol, grimacing as he swallows. "Your tastes have certainly changed; no longer a top-shelf man?"

Without looking away, I say, "A lot of things have changed, and it gets the job done. Now, why did you want to meet?"

My father levels a calculating gaze on me. I can see when he decides not to bullshit me. "Come home. People are talking, and it's been bad for business. Shareholders are balking that you aren't there, and many of the clients you brought in don't want to work with your replacement."

I lean back, crossing my arms over my chest. "No."

"What do you mean, no? I've been more than patient with you. This ridiculous tantrum you're throwing. Grow up; you're a thirty-two-year-old man, for god's sake."

"I'm thirty-three." Is it petulant to call him out for getting my goddamn age wrong? "It's not a tantrum. It's me doing what *I* want for the first time. I'm sorry you can't respect or understand that. But, no, I won't be coming back."

"Think of your mother. You ran off without a word. For all we knew, something terrible could have happened to you."

"Given that I've been in contact with HR to take care of my off-boarding and final paycheck, I'm certain you were aware of where I've been."

My father snarls out his answer. "Yes, with Tuesday in that hellhole of a town. How could you turn your back on the company? On our family? You've taken everything I've provided for you and tossed it in my face. You and your sister."

I grit my teeth and force my knuckles to release their death grip on my glass. "Don't talk about Tuesday. You don't deserve her name on your lips. And the little *hellhole,* as you call it, has been a fucking sanctuary compared to what I left behind." My temper flares, and my voice rises. "I thought I made it clear in December that I was done. And again, now, when I said no. But in case it wasn't, I'm done with Phillips Construction. Done with you. Done with this pitiful excuse for a family."

"You think you're so goddamn smart, don't you?"

People say Tuesday and I have our father's eyes, but I don't see it. Our eyes resemble golden whiskey, a warm brown; his are nothing but hard, frozen amber. Unyielding. Unchanging.

"This was a mistake." I say it as much for myself as him.

"No, the only mistake was you siding with Tuesday and then running away from the consequences of your actions. As if the two of you matter to one another." He keeps going, his face twisted in a hateful sneer. "You can make me out to be the bad guy all you want, but you stood by me for years while your sister was pushed aside. Do you think she'll ever forgive you? Really?"

I sit in stunned silence as he continues his tirade. "Look at you; you're a disgrace. A mess. Throwing years of schooling and connections away and for what? You're no one's hero."

He leans back, radiating superiority. Shame roils in my stomach, churning alongside the bourbon. I don't have a counterpoint because he's right.

My phone quietly hums in my pocket. Grateful for any excuse to look away from my father's cold, wolfish face, I pull it out.

> **TUESDAY**
> Love you too, War. We miss you. Good luck tonight.

Attached is a picture of Tuesday, Bond, and their friends smiling and flashing thumbs-up signs.

Without saying another word, I rise from the booth, take off my watch, and lay it and a couple of twenties on the table.

"Wh-what do you think you're doing?" My father sputters, red dots coloring his cheeks.

"Whatever I want. Maybe I'll catch a rodeo." And with that, I walk out of the bar.

CHAPTER NINE
Laramie

Lubbock, Texas
March

The High Plains Stampede isn't the most glamorous return to the glory of racing. Houston or Ft. Worth would have been much bigger splashes, but Dr. Panter and I agreed early on that March was my best chance of being back in riding form.

Given the way things have gone so far, though, I kind of wish I'd listened to her at my last appointment when she suggested I give it another week or two. Sighing, I rotate my sore shoulder while I pace in front of X's stall. My practice runs today—and in the weeks leading up to today—have been... well, abysmal might be too kind a word.

This morning's first run-through started with a bad approach to the first barrel. I was too wide, and we never got our momentum back. The second run was more of the same. It's been everything from my body position to poor timing with the reins, and it all screams rookie riding in her first show, not a veteran returning from a small break. I've made more mistakes in the past few hours than I have since my debut.

I can't get my mind right, no matter how many breathing exercises I do or how much I berate myself.

Even Xpresso is frustrated with me. As if sensing my thoughts, she pops her head over the stall door, her pinned-back ears flickering.

Opening the latch, I step into her space. "I know, girl. I'm trying. I swear." Resting my forehead against the warm curve of her neck, I let her steady breathing ground me. She doesn't judge me when I wrap an arm around her withers and cling tighter. "I fucked up, X." My voice drops to a whisper. "I never should have left him."

It's not the first time I've shared my secrets and shames with her. This one, in particular, has been a constant over the last twelve weeks. From the second I slipped out of that warm bed at The Rusty Spur, leaving War behind, I've regretted it.

When I slunk through the front door that morning, I ran to my dad and cried in his arms. Something I hadn't done in years. He, of course, thought I was injured. How did I explain I *was* hurt, but it was all my own doing?

I still can't explain it to myself. One night with him, and I was crying? My heart was aching? I missed him? It was ridiculous. *So* not me. And yet, there I was, sobbing on my dad's shoulder, wishing I could go back to the motel and make it right.

The words my father said to me still ring in my ears. *"Mimi, if life has taught me anything, it's that connections come when you least expect them, but if you find one, you don't let it go. You chase it and hope you can keep it."*

So I did. I put on my big girl pants and cowgirled up. I wiped my tears away and sped back to The Rusty Spur, ready to apologize and explain why I left. Ask him if we could go out again. Tell him how much I wanted to get to know him, to find out if this spark between us could grow into a fire. But he was gone, the bed cold, and the clothes I'd bought him for our date left behind.

The following week, I asked Dr. Panter about him, my regret growing when she admitted he hadn't returned to her office. I not-so-delicately tried to get his phone number or address from our shared doctor, but she rightfully declined my request.

Did I maybe go a little to the dark side and stalk his socials, looking for any clues I could find about where he might live? Yes. Am I proud of it? No. But only because it didn't yield any results. I found out where his condo was, but when the sweet doorman informed me *Mr. Phillips* had sold his penthouse, I knew it was time to let it go.

I'm not so vain that I think he sold his home because of me—or at least not just because of me. But it makes me wonder how much I didn't know about him and what else was happening in his life. It also adds to the guilt I carry.

After finding out he was really gone, I put on my best media face—a fake grin that doesn't meet my eyes—and poured all my energy and attention into meeting my goals.

But instead of improving, my sessions got worse. I was singularly focused on my exercises but fervently so. I spent hours outside of PT working my arm. I pushed myself so hard I ended up losing ground rather than gaining it and re-injured my shoulder in mid-January. I had to beg Dr. Panter to sign off on my paperwork to be able to compete this week.

If she could see how I'm pushing my shoulder now, she'd have my head.

X nickers and nudges me. The warm sound pulls me from my memories. Sighing, I slip her a peppermint. "Thanks for being such a good listener. I promise tonight will go better."

Only because it can't go worse.

I go through the grounding motions of getting X ready for the race: giving her one last brush down and then tacking her up. As I work, I talk to her, praising and assuring her that we've got this.

Once she's ready, I slide the stall door open and guide her toward the warm-up area. As we walk, I avoid the eyes of those around me. I'm not in the mood for small talk, for false interest in how I've been, or for faux concern over the state of my practice runs. Though I wish my dad wasn't in his seat, I could use a friendly face.

From my vantage point, I can see the stands, so I do a quick scan, looking for my dad. Even a wave from him would go a long way, but a flash of reddish-brown hair under the arena lights catches my eye.

Butterflies swarm my stomach at the thought it could be him. A pang of longing pounds in my chest as I study the mystery man. His back is to me, allowing me to take in the shoulders that are broad enough to belong to my Pretty Boy. But the shaggy hair, work clothes, and thicker build tell me it's another flight of fancy on my part.

I wilt a little. Even after three months, I search for him everywhere I go. Each time a patient walked into the PT room, any time a fancy car pulled through the gates at Prairie Sky Equine, every time the door blew open at Stir-ups, I held my breath, hoping it was him. It was wishful thinking then, and it's certainly wishful now. There's a less than zero chance War Philips is in Lubbock, much less at the High Plains Stampede. And even if it was him, it's not like he'd want to see me. That sobering thought pulls me back to reality.

Get over it, Laramie. You made the choice, and now you have to live with it.

Rolling my neck and cracking my knuckles, I push War and my regrets from my mind. I owe it to myself and to Xpresso to be here, be present. Turning back to my horse, I smile, a real one. "Alright, you boss bitch, let's show them we're back."

Xpresso's steps are sure when she enters the alley. I visualize the course one last time, mentally correcting the many, many mistakes I made earlier in the day. In my mind, X and I flow like water, floating around the turns, rushing through the straightaways. The way it should be.

When the gate handler calls my number, I inhale, letting the familiar scents settle over me. It's been too long. *Horsehair. Saddle oil. Dirt. Home.* The last bit of tension in my shoulders melts away. This is where I belong.

At the sound of the buzzer, we burst forward like a bullet shot from a gun. I let years of muscle memory take over and trust X to do what needs to be done. We round the first barrel without problem. I subtly shift my weight, following the glide of X's muscles as we sprint toward the next turn. The world around us fades to nothing. We aren't perfect, but the connection between us, that silent bond we've honed over the years, comes roaring back.

It's just Xpresso and me: a girl and her horse.

"Laramie, someone wants to speak with you." My dad's warm voice calls to me from outside the stable.

Without looking up, I say, "One sec, Dad." I pat X once more, then slip her an apple. "You kicked ass tonight, lady."

After all the disastrous run-throughs, the pain of months of rehab, the regret of letting War go, we did it. It wasn't our fastest time, but we qualified for night two.

I straighten my shirt, stomp some of the manure off my boots, and sigh. "I hope this isn't a new potential sponsor. I'm not up to kissing ass tonight."

X snorts in solidarity. Or at least that's my interpretation.

Dusting off my hands, I slide the door closed behind me. "Who wants—" The words die in my throat. Standing before me is the man I glimpsed earlier. The one my heart jumped at, but my brain immediately dismissed. My breath catches in my lungs. It can't be.

The reddish brown hair that was so neat now spills over the collar of his plaid flannel. Gone is the pricey watch, leaving a band of pale skin against his otherwise tan wrist. His broad shoulders still cut an imposing line, though his waist is less tapered than before. Daring to hope, I lift my gaze higher to his face. And though much of it hides under a messy beard, there's no denying those honey-brown eyes.

It's him.

Like a top in motion, everything spins, and all I manage is one strangled word. "War?"

He stares at me like I might disappear and then smiles. "Congratulations, Trouble."

CHAPTER TEN

war

After storming out on my father, I debate my next steps for about four seconds. I could go back to Trail Creek or chase a long shot. Something spurs me toward the impossible. It reminds me of the same internal urging that prompted me to stand up for Tuesday, to tell my parents I was quitting, to say yes to a date with Laramie, and to walk out on my father tonight.

I'm learning to trust my instincts, and it isn't the time to doubt myself.

So I drive the thirty minutes to the outskirts of Lubbock and the midsize arena hosting The High Plains Stampede, wondering if, on a scale of one to bat-crap bananas, what the chances are that Laramie is here. The practical side of me calculates the odds at just this side of finding out the moon is actually made of cheese.

Still, I can't deny being in her element makes me feel more connected to her, even if it's a tenuous thread at best.

There are way more people here than I expect, but thankfully, they have plenty of seats available. I splurge and buy one near the racing gate rather than the chutes—which matters if you want to see the racers. The nice lady in the ticket booth explained all this after she asked me where I wanted to sit, and I stared at her like she'd grown an extra head.

Sliding past the occupied seats, I find mine and plop down next to an older man.

"Hey, there." He greets me with a kind smile.

I dip my head in greeting before looking for any sign of Laramie. A roster, her name, anything.

"First time at a rodeo?" the man asks.

My lips tug upwards. "What gave me away?"

He shrugs. "I can spot a greenhorn." There's a teasing tone to his words that appeals to me.

Leaning closer to him, I say, "So I'm guessing you're an old hand?" At his nod, I continue. "Any chance you know how I can find out who's competing in the barrel races?"

He hums. "I can." His piercing brown eyes study me. "Who you looking for?"

"Laramie Larson. She may not—"

A large work-worn hand lands on my bad shoulder, and I give a slight wince. His lips quirk in a small smile. "Son, you're in exactly the right place, especially if you're who I think you are."

A thousand thoughts flicker through my mind when I see her. *How have you been? How's your shoulder? Are you seeing anyone? Why did you leave me that night?*

That one, more than any other, echoes over and over.

But all I manage to say is, "Congratulations, Trouble," before thin arms loop around my waist and a head of beautiful brown hair presses to my chest.

The last thing I expect is a hug; the shock and her unexpected weight are enough to knock me down, taking Laramie with me. We end up in a pile on the ground, my back flat against the dirt and her wide-eyed, looking down at me.

"Shit, I'm sorry!" Laramie blurts as I say, "Be careful of your shoulder."

I breathe in her scent, that mix of hay, sunshine, and the sweeter undercurrent of a fresh bouquet. My hands drift to her hips, and for another beat, we lay there, staring at each other. Being this close to her sends a pang of longing through me.

"What are you doing here?" Laramie brushes a too-long strand off my forehead, searching my face as if she can't believe I'm real. *The feeling's mutual, sweetheart.*

"Mimi, you wanna let the man up?" Her dad's laugh snaps us to action.

"Oh, crap, yeah." Laramie scrambles off me before reaching to help me up.

Once we're back on our feet, an awkward silence settles over us, neither of us able to tear our eyes away, but both frozen in place. I want to go to her, to gather her into my arms and shake her while begging her to tell me why she left and how I can make her stay. Spank her ass for putting me through all this pain and then kiss it all better. Get on my knees and promise to be so good for her, she'll never think of running from me again. Fuck her into the mattress so deep, she can't walk away.

Conflicted might be the best way to describe what I'm feeling. And if the cloud of indecision flickering across her face is any indication, it's the same for her.

From behind us, Kit chuckles. "I think you two have some things to discuss."

"How do you..." Laramie gestures between her father and me, her brow furrowed.

"I'll let the young man here fill you in on all that." He steps up to Laramie and hugs her. "You did good, Mimi. Tomorrow will be even better. I'll see you back at the trailer. Be safe. Be smart."

To me, he extends a hand. "War, think about what I said."

The older man's words replay. *"She spent weeks crying over you and her mistake. I don't tell you that to make you feel any kind of way. My Mimi, she's a tough girl, but she's also soft. She just buries it down. Not pushing you to give her another chance, but you being here... well, that says it all. I wasted years hiding my feelings for Laramie's mom when I could have been hers. Pretending she was nothing but a friend. I'd give almost anything to have those years back. Years I could have spent showing her how much I loved her."*

That I ended up seated next to the father of the woman I'd spent the past three months obsessing over—while adamantly trying to convince myself I was not obsessed—was like a gift from the universe. A universe with a weird, fucked-up sense of humor, but I'll take it.

I take her hand in mine. "You were amazing."

Some of the tension melts from her shoulders, and she gives me a cocky smirk. "If you think I was good tonight, just wait."

A layer of innuendo threads into her words, but I'm not here to sleep with her. Or at least not *just* to sleep with her.

The teasing smile falls from her lips, and she shuffles her boots in the dirt. "How do you know my dad? How are you here?"

"Is there somewhere we can sit?"

Laramie looks around as if realizing we're still in the

holding area of the arena. She nods. "Yeah. Let's grab some food."

I follow behind her as she picks her way between trailers and pop-up tents until she finds one serving barbecue. She grabs us a plate to share, then jerks her head toward an empty table. We sit across from each other, and another wave of uncomfortable silence hangs between us.

"I was in—"

"What are you—"

It's not the first time we've broken the tension by speaking at the same time, and it works again. Both of us relax, sending the other coy smiles.

Crunching a chip, Laramie waves her hand, encouraging me to speak.

"You asked me a few questions, Trouble. Which one do you want answered first?"

Raising one eyebrow, she says, "My dad. How did you end up with him? Phillips Construction bought Biscuit—Grand Dominion—from us, but that was all handled through a third party, so it isn't from that."

"I don't, or I didn't." I pick at the brisket on the plate. "I ended up sitting next to him randomly."

Laramie's mouth drops open. "Hundreds of people, and you end up next to my dad?"

Pushing the food out of the way, I reach across the table, resting my hand over hers. She flips it so we're palm to palm, and I rub my thumb over her inner wrist. "I couldn't believe it either. He loves bragging about you." A mix of warmth and jealousy grows in my stomach. Has my father ever been proud enough to talk about me to a stranger?

The pink that darkens her cheeks is gorgeous. I wasn't sure she was capable of blushing, but now that I know she can, I'm going to do everything in my power to make it happen over and over.

"Yeah, he's my biggest fan." Despite her attempt at downplaying it, I can tell she's pleased.

"As he should be," I whisper so quietly I'm not sure if Laramie hears me, but then her eyes snap to mine.

"Why are you here?" she asks again.

"For you, Trouble."

Her sharp gasp makes me wonder if I've played my cards too soon. I watch her swallow, waiting her out.

When she finally speaks, it's so faint I have to strain to catch what she says. "You have no idea how happy I am to hear that." Laramie pulls our hands to her mouth, placing a chaste kiss on my knuckles. "So do you, um, want to—"

"How do you feel about breakfast?" I interrupt to keep her from asking me to go somewhere right now. I'm not strong enough to turn her down if she invites me into her bed, but I'm doing things my way this time. Getting to know her, making it so she can't bear to run from me again.

Her face crinkles in confusion. "Breakfast?"

"Yeah, it's this meal people eat in the morning. Maybe you've heard of it?"

She narrows her eyes at me. "And you call me a smart ass?"

Grinning, I say, "On my way into town, I kept seeing billboards for some famous pancake place."

"The Stacks? You don't want to eat there. It's all a marketing gimmick. The real best pancakes in town are at Lulu's."

I rise from the table, make my way around to her, and guide her to her feet. Once she's standing, I reach down and tuck a lock of wild brown hair behind her ear. "Sure am glad I ran into you. I'd hate to have come all this way and eaten subpar pancakes."

"Yeah, that'd be a real shame." Her voice is sultry, and she steps closer as if drawn by an invisible string.

"I don't know my way around here; any chance you might"—I take a deep breath and forge on—"want to go with me in the morning? To make sure I get there okay?"

A smile tugs at her lips. "That's all?"

My hands move of their own accord, unable to resist holding her when she's this close. One arm wraps around her lower back; the other goes to her nape. "Maybe a few other reasons, too."

"Like what?"

"Like getting to know you."

"Without tequila and steak fingers."

"Without tequila and steak fingers," I agree.

"Give me your phone." I adore her bossy ass. Though I hate to take my hands off her, I comply, unlocking my phone and passing it to her.

Her thumbs fly over the screen before she tosses it back to me. "I added my information and texted myself. I'll pick you up at eight?"

"No, sweetheart. I'll pick *you* up at eight."

She nibbles her bottom lip, that pretty blush faint on her cheeks. "Well, alright then. I guess I'll see you in the morning." Laramie rises onto her tip-toes and brushes her lips against mine. It's a whisper of a kiss, but it's also a promise of more. A promise I'm clinging to.

"Sleep tight, Trouble." With one last squeeze of her hips, I turn and walk away, lighter than I've been in months.

I shift on the uncomfortable motel mattress, rereading Laramie's texts for the hundredth time.

> **YOUR TROUBLE**
> Now you can chase me if I run 😉
>
> Too soon?

That she entered her name as *Your Trouble* had my heart jumping. God, how I want it to be true, for her to be mine. My trouble. My future.

My phone buzzes, a new text adding to the thread.

> I really am sorry, War. I'm looking forward to breakfast and a chance to talk.
>
> Me too, sweetheart. Get some sleep.

When Laramie doesn't answer after a few minutes, I figure she's taken my advice and turned in for the night. Switching gears, I brace myself to share the night's developments with my sister and pull up our text thread.

> Things with Dad went about as well as you'd expect
>
> **TUESDAY**
> 😉 I hate to say I told you so, mostly because I can't because you didn't tell me you were doing this, but...
>
> I deserve that
>
> Can we talk?

No sooner than I send the last text does my phone ring. "Hey."

"What's wrong?" Tuesday asks, somehow able to read me even from that one word.

"Hi to you, too, sis." I chuckle, but Tuesday isn't deterred.

"War." My name is a warning. A warmth spreads through me that someone cares enough to scold me.

I draw in a long breath. "Do you want the bad news or the weird news?"

"Bad news first. Then we'll move on to weird."

"The meeting with Dad was a clusterfuck."

"What happened?"

I shrug despite her not being able to see it. "More of the same. Scare tactics and threats when I didn't immediately agree to return to Dallas and Phillips Construction." My voice drops. "I left my watch with him."

"What? You love that thing. I mean, I think it's ostentatious, but for the last three years, you've never taken it off."

A strangled laugh slips from my throat. "Tonight, I realized it was more of a shackle than a showpiece."

"What happened after that?"

"I walked out." I run my hand through my hair. "The picture you sent... you didn't plan it, but it gave me the courage to leave. So, thank you." I swallow. "Tuesday, I doubt I'll ever be able to do enough to make things right for all the hurt I caused you, but I won't ever stop trying."

Over the line, she sniffles. "I've told you, there's nothing to forgive. You stood up for me when I needed you the most, and you've been by my side since then. We didn't have a normal upbringing. I don't blame you for doing what you felt you had to. You're a good man, Warren Phillips."

I rest the heel of my palm over my heart where my sister's kind words have settled. Aiming to lighten the mood, I groan and say, "Don't call me Warren."

She giggles. "Fine, fine. Okay, I'm ready for the weird. Spill it."

"So, I'm extending my stay in Lubbock by a few days."

"What? Why?"

"Do you remember the day I showed up in Trail Creek?"

"Of course. You were a wreck."

"And the night we went to The Great Dane and you convinced me to drink three Flocked Up Flamingos?"

Her laugh makes me smile. "God, yes. You were a mess." Her laughter cuts off. "Oh. Laramie."

"Yep."

"She's there?" Surprise colors Tuesday's voice.

"Believe me, I'm as shocked as you are."

"How did you... when did..." She sputters before finally settling on, "What?"

I chuckle. "After leaving the bar, I drove to some arena and somehow ended up sitting next to Kit Larson, her dad."

"Damn. What are the odds?" She pauses before continuing. "War, that's a sign if I've ever heard one."

Closing my eyes, I say, "I'm scared out of my mind." Being vulnerable with Tuesday is new, but after the way I crawled to her back in December, it's safe to say she's seen me at my worst.

"You're a moron if you don't take advantage of this."

My mouth is like parchment. "What if I do this and she leaves again?" Confessing that fear loosens some of the tightness in my chest.

"What if you don't do this and miss out on something amazing?" Tuesday counters before huffing out a sharp laugh. "You and I have more in common than we know. Do you think I didn't try to run from Bond? To deny what I felt for him? That I wasn't scared? But he's everything I've ever wanted, and I never would have gotten it if I hadn't taken a chance." Her tone softens. "What would you regret more?"

What would I regret more? Having her for only a moment or never having her at all?

The answer is easy.

With renewed clarity, I say my goodbyes to my sister. Shutting off the lamp, I slide my arms behind my head and stare into the dark. A smile tugs at my lips as I drift off to sleep. Tomorrow, I take steps toward the future I want.

CHAPTER ELEVEN
Laramie

I step into my trailer and fling myself onto the small sofa next to my dad.

"You're back earlier than I expected." He raises one graying eyebrow at me.

"Want to tell me what all you and the man I spent the last three months mooning over talked about?" I playfully scold him for blindsiding me.

Dad takes a draw from his long neck and huffs. "Nope."

"No?" I repeat, my mouth dropping open.

"You two need to talk things out. I did my part in getting him back to see you."

I slump against the cushions and cross my arms over my chest. "Fine. At least tell me how he was during my run."

"Mesmerized, Mimi. Absolutely mesmerized."

Something bright and fizzy rises from my stomach before settling in my heart. It reminds me of my first sip of champagne, filling all the empty places inside me, swelling and welling until I burst.

A line of tears trickle down my cheeks, and I hasten to

scrub them away. Scoffing, I say, "Of course he was. I'm awesome." My voice cracks on the last word, belying my bravado.

The warm comfort of my father's hug wraps around me. "Damn straight."

"Ugh, okay, okay. Enough sniveling." I fan my face and laugh while snagging Dad's beer to finish it off. After a beat, I murmur, "He's taking me to breakfast in the morning."

When my dad doesn't respond, I glance at him and catch him staring at me with a soft, goofy smile.

"What?"

"Nothing, Mimi. Just like seeing you like this."

"A crying mess? You didn't get enough of that back in December? And January? And—"

"These tears are different. You've got that gleam in your eyes, your spark."

I shrug. "I'm a nervous wreck. What if I mess up again?"

"Then you apologize again." Dad chucks my chin. "Nothing's permanent until you're six feet under. If you want this to work with him, you'll make it happen."

Whispering, I ask what's been on my mind since I saw War. "Can we make it work? I travel so much. We're so different..."

Dad is the only one who sees this side of me. The world gets the brash, bold, wild parts. Kit Larson gets the rest.

He weighs his words before answering. "If there's one thing that's always been true about you, you go after and get what you want. If War is it, it'll work out. I have no doubts about that. But, Mimi, you have to be all in. No relationship can survive if you have a foot out the door or are looking for a reason to run."

"How'd you get to be so smart?"

"Well, I've been around the sun a few times. I traded my

good looks for all the experience that comes with age. Plus, I had your mom. She taught me everything I know."

"I miss her." Though Mom's been gone over ten years, I still wish she was here. For moments like this, to watch me race, for my dad.

He squeezes my shoulder. "Me too. She'd like War."

I arch an eyebrow. "How do you know that? Did you two bond while I was racing?"

"Only over you. But she'd like him because you do." Dad's knees creak as he rises off the tiny loveseat. "You take the bed; you need your beauty sleep."

A snort pulls from my lips. "Ha! Good one, old man. I heard every bone in your body crack when you got up. I'll pull out the sofa."

He hesitates like he's ready to argue, but when I jut out my chin, he knows I won't bend.

Waving a hand, Dad says, "Alright, you stubborn mule. I'll take the big bed tonight, but tomorrow I'll get a hotel. In case you, um, need privacy."

I cover my face with my hands. "Oh my god, Dad. Stop. Right now. Before I die and never get to go to breakfast with War or win a title."

"Interesting order you put those in."

It takes me a second to process what he means. Then it hits me: I put a date with War before winning the NRF, and it bothers me way less than I expect.

It's five till eight, and War isn't here. I pace back and forth in front of the arena entrance, self-soothing with the fact he's not late. Not yet, anyway.

I scan the parking lot, searching for a flashy sports car. I have no idea what he drives, but I'm sure it's high end. A horrible thought grips me as I make my tenth circuit from one end of the entry gate to the other. What if this is payback for leaving him alone in Mel's motel?

He wouldn't plan all this just to stand me up. Right? I mean, I wouldn't blame him... No. I shake all those doubts from my head. He's coming. He wants to see me. To get to know me.

At eight on the dot, a slate gray Bronco pulls up to the curb, and War hops out.

"You ready to go, Trouble?" he asks as he opens the passenger door for me.

Like an idiot, I stand on the sidewalk, looking from him to the expensive SUV and back. He groomed his beard and styled his hair away from his face. He's casually dressed but already looks more like the man I met in Dallas.

Not that he wasn't delicious as a rumpled mountain man.

I blurt, "You trimmed your beard."

War rubs his hand over his chin. "Yeah, it was getting out of hand. I hadn't done anything to it in, um, well, since..." He trails off then gives me a sheepish grin. "My sister says I look like a yeti. She'll be thrilled I pared it back."

Stepping into his space, I run my fingers over the soft hair. "I like it. You look rugged."

"So, not your Pretty Boy anymore?"

The use of *your* isn't lost on me, and my heart skips a beat. "You'll always be my Pretty Boy." I breathe the words against his lips. When did we get so close?

A sound—half moan, half growl—rumbles up from War's chest, and then his hands are on my hips, anchoring me to him. The kiss is all-consuming. Fervent. He savors my lips as if I hold every truth he's ever searched for.

I don't care that it's eight in the morning. That we're standing in the parking lot of a rodeo arena in Lubbock. That we have so much to figure out. All I know is this man is mine, and I'm not letting him go.

War breaks the kiss with a curse. "Shit, sweetheart." He rests his forehead against mine. "I wasn't planning to do that."

"Kiss me?"

"At least not until I fed you."

My fingers trace up his nape and grasp the hair at his collar. "Then let's get me fed." With a wink, I hop into the passenger seat and raise my eyebrows at him. "Coming?"

He barks out a loud laugh. "Such a smart ass." The door shuts, and I appreciate the way he jogs around the car. Those extra pounds look good on him.

We get about a mile down the road, both of us making silly, meaningless chit-chat. It's nice—less awkward standing around the pool and more dipping a toe in the water.

Then War dives into the deep end. "So, what's the sleeping situation?"

I put a teasing lilt to my voice and shift closer. "Trying to get lucky already? I thought we agreed to eat first."

"You don't have to swing at every pitch, you know."

Grinning, I reach out and squeeze his thigh. "Where's the fun in that?"

"You're incorrigible."

"You mispronounced incredible." This earns me a choked laugh that has him beating on his chest to clear his lungs.

Once he's breathing, he laces his fingers with mine. "Okay, really, though. Where do you sleep when you're competing?"

"My trailer has living quarters. It's small but functional. Sometimes, Dad stays with me; sometimes, he gets a hotel. He, uh, made sure to tell me he'd be getting one tonight." I fight the blush trying to spread over my cheeks.

War stares at me a beat then shakes his head. "And you travel, what'd you say, two hundred days a year?"

"Give or take. It depends on how many big events are happening and how the season's going. If I bank enough points early on and the purses are small, then it's less. If I'm straggling or want the money, then it's more."

War's jaw tightens, and his hand flexes around mine. "I see."

Before I can unpack those two words, we pull into Lulu's. I don't wait for War to come around and open my door, which is apparently the wrong thing to do.

"Laramie, I swear. Can't you let me be a gentleman?"

I freeze, half out of the Bronco. "Want me to climb back in?"

He sighs. "No. Can I at least get the door to the restaurant for you?"

"Yes. And I promise I won't fight you for the bill. How's that?"

"A start." He's adorably grumpy. Happy War, annoyed War, just came inside me War. How can I pick a favorite?

His lips twitch when we step into Lulu's, but he doesn't say anything about the uneven floors, rough-hewn walls, or twangy Texas country piping over the speakers.

The waitress leads us to a small table near the window, but I wave her off when she offers menus. "We'll take..." As soon as I start to order, I pause. "Actually, could we have a few minutes?"

War studies me. "Were you about to order for us?"

I duck, inhale, and straighten. "Is my independence a problem for you? I'm not used to being a passenger princess."

He swallows, and for a heartbeat, I fear the worst. I'm too much. He can't give up control any more than I can.

"If we're moving forward, we both have to give." He leans toward me, crooking his finger. When our faces are mere inches apart, he says, "It's hot as hell when you take charge, but sometimes, I need to take care of you."

A piece of me melts. Could I handle that? Giving up power, letting War lead the way? I wait for my twin devils to chime in, to scream for me to cut and run, but they're silent.

Maybe it's time to let someone other than my dad see the fragile parts of me.

"And taking care of me entails what?" I ask. This is all new territory for me.

Warm fingers feather over my lips and down my neck. "Little things like opening doors, paying." I go to argue, but he shushes me. "Paying when I ask you out; being there when you're scared or sad." His honey eyes darken. "Worshipping you in bed."

Closing the space between us, I kiss him, grinning when his eyes widen in surprise. "I think we can work something out."

The waitress clears her throat, breaking the tension between us. War lays the menu on the table and gestures to me. "She's the one you want."

Like a fuzzy blanket on a chilly day, his small offering warms me inside and out. And when the chocolate chip and pecan pancakes arrive, he agrees they're the best he's ever had.

Belly full, I rest on my elbows and watch War eat. "So you have a sister?"

"Yes. She's my twin."

"Oh, that's so cool! I always wanted siblings, but it wasn't in the cards. You guys must be close."

Pain flickers across War's face. "We've gotten closer in the past few months."

I cock my head, giving him wait time. He pushes the last few bites of his breakfast around his plate, looking everywhere but at me.

"Is this more of a third-date conversation?" I ask, giving him an out if he wants it.

He rewards me with a half-smile. "No. It's just, well, it doesn't paint me in the best light."

Reaching across the table, I wrap my fingers around his bare wrist. "Does it have anything to do with your missing watch? Or how the heck you ended up in Lubbock? Or why you sold your apart—" I snap my mouth shut.

War hums and lifts his eyebrows. "We'll circle back to how you know I sold my apartment." The teasing tone fades as he goes on. "There's a lot to it; some of it isn't mine to share, but my family is..."

"Complicated?"

"Shitty."

His wry reply pulls an unexpected laugh from me that I try to stifle as I signal for the check. I catch his scowl and put my hands up in surrender. "Not paying, just thought maybe you'd want to have this conversation somewhere else? You can hang out with Xpresso and me while I get her ready."

"Won't I be in the way?"

"Not if you listen to me." Butter wouldn't melt in my mouth; I'm so sweet.

"T-r-o-u-b-l-e. With a capital T." There's no heat in his

words, and he's pressing his lips together, concealing his smile. "Alright. You win."

He makes quick work of the check and great time back to the arena. I flash my credentials and hook my arm with War's, leading him to the staging area. It's my favorite kind of chaos back here. Riders, handlers, event officials, vets, and staff mingle, weaving around rough stock and thoroughbred horses that cost as much as a car.

It feeds my energy and my nerves.

Together, we pick our way toward the stalls where Xpresso waits. Her ears prick, and she lets out a nicker when she senses me.

"Hey, X. I brought a friend."

As if sizing him up, X sniffs War's extended arm. Then she gives a soft snort and nuzzles against him.

"Oh, she likes you."

"She does?" War sounds years younger.

"Yep. There's this asshole rider, Cyrus McClain, the first time he met Xpresso—uninvited, by the way—she nipped him good and then let out this squeal that I swear could've busted windows."

I guide War's hand to her withers and mirror how to stroke her. It isn't long before her eyes drift closed, and she leans into his touch. *Yeah, I feel ya, girl.*

With War enraptured by Xpresso, I work on prepping her for the day, leaving him to talk.

"So, you were saying things with your family are complicated?"

War chuffs. "I said shitty. But yeah. We aren't winning Family of the Year anytime soon." He pauses. "Though my mom would be all about that if it existed."

I quirk a brow, encouraging him to go on. X nudges him as well.

"Tuesday—my sister—and I... I'm sure you know the kind of family we grew up in."

"Yeah, one that can afford one of my dad's horses."

"With that came a lot of trappings and expectations. Impossible ones for Tuesday and almost impossible for me."

Squatting, I check X's hooves. "What do you mean?"

He goes to touch his wrist, but when he finds it bare, he runs his free hand through his hair. "My parents held us both to ridiculous standards, but no matter what Tuesday did, it was never good enough. I, um, I got caught up in ambition and the desire to be better. And I hurt the one person I should've been there for."

"Hurt her how?"

His shoulders curl forward, and, while War Phillips isn't a small man, he seems to have shrunk. "Not standing up for her. Watching my father and mother bully and berate her over every fucking thing. I put the business before her when she needed me." His voice catches. "I helped them send her away."

Xpresso stiffens, picking up on the tension radiating from War, so I step away from her flank and put myself where she can see me. I offer her an apple slice and soothe her muzzle. Once she's settled, I press myself to War's back, wrapping my arms around him.

My voice is soft when I say, "But you're growing closer now? Tell me about that."

He turns, hugging me closer. "Around the time you and I met, I finally did the right thing. I backed Tuesday's play, and we screwed my dad over." He smiles into my hair. "I won't ever forget the look on his face when he realized he lost." There's a pause, but as I'm about to break away, War tightens his grip. "The day you and I went out, I told my parents I was done with them. I was done letting them push me around. Done listening to them bad-mouth Tuesday. Just done."

"That's why you were late?"

"Yep." He chuckles. "Then I had the best date of my life."

My heart sinks. "And I left you."

War lets out a heavy sigh, and his voice drops. "And you left me."

It's my turn to cling to him—a desperate barnacle, cleaving myself to a mooring. "I'm so sorry, War. I never should have run."

"In a way, I owe you a thanks."

I peer up at him, trying to parse out what he's saying.

"If you hadn't ditched me..." *Ouch.* "I never would have sold my apartment and run to Trail Creek. Which means I wouldn't have met my father in Lubbock and ended up at a rodeo."

My thoughts tumble, and I fidget against War's hold. "So, I'm the reason we're together now?"

A smirk tugs at his full lips. "That's one way to look at it." He presses his forehead to mine. "I would love to have those three months spent without you back, but I'm so fucking glad I'm here now."

X whinnies and stamps as we wait for our turn. After War left, his parting words played like a record stuck on repeat. A flurry of nerves came to life in X's stall this morning, and the bastards refuse to settle. Instead, they swoop and dive and belly-flop their way through my system, searching out any ounce of calm and mutating it until all I'm made of is jitters.

He's glad he's here. He actually *is* here. He wishes we could've had those three months.

My twin devils are at a loss. If he shouted or ended things, they'd be ablaze. That's territory they thrive in. But here, in this new place—where a man like War kisses the tip of my nose, hugs me, forgives me—they have nothing to say.

And it's incredibly disquieting.

X takes two steps before I get her back in the lane. She's feeding off the wonky energy I'm putting out. I breathe in for five and hold it for six. Then do it again. I've got to get myself under control.

Don't think about War being in the audience, sitting with Dad, watching me ride. Wanting more.

Focus, Laramie! I'm last tonight, and the posted times are respectable. Not great, but good. I'm better. If X and I run clean, we'll make it to tomorrow night and a chance for the purse.

Like a shot, the timer starts, and X races through the gate. We come in to turn one a wide but quickly adjust. Turn two goes smoothly, but at turn three, it all falls apart. My shoulder locks, and I jerk the reins in response, pulling X too close to the barrel. Her flank catches it, and I know without looking, we just earned a five-second penalty. The silence of the audience confirms it. We sprint through the straightaway, but the damage is done.

I blew it.

Again.

CHAPTER TWELVE

war

My knee bounces as I wait for the barrel racing event to begin. Right now, a dozen adorable kids in mini Western wear ride sheep all around the arena.

"Mutton bustin'," Kit says to my unasked question.

"Did Laramie do that when she was young?"

"Sure did." Pride seeps from him. "Until it got too boring for her, then she was off on the back of a horse."

It's easy to picture a little Laramie demanding to ride a horse over a lamb. "She's not scared of much, is she?"

Kit mulls over my words. "She puts on a brave face. Now, don't get me wrong, my daughter would chase lightning in a tin suit if the mood struck her, but there's plenty that scares her."

I wait for him to go on, watching as he presses his lips into a thin line. "Mimi lost her mom when she was sixteen. That's a hard time for a girl, hell, any kid, to lose a parent. I did my best, but her past relationships haven't been worth writing home about." He rubs the stubble on his jaw. "I'm not gonna say anything else because that's between you and her, but don't let her daring keep you from seeing the rest of her."

With a grunt, Kit stands. "I'm gonna grab a beer. You want one?"

At my nod, he leaves me alone, pondering his words. I still have so much to learn about Laramie, and I hope she gives me the time and opportunity to do it. The connection between us, the feelings I have for her are fast and maybe irresponsible, but it's more than lust. The puzzle that is Laramie Larson somehow grows clearer and murkier.

While I wait, the cute kids finish riding—and falling off—their sheep. The announcer blares over the speakers, sharing the next event's lineup.

"Ladies and gentlemen, get ready to be on the edge of your seats! Our talented round-two barrel racers and their horses will compete against the clock and each other to secure a spot in tomorrow's finals! Let's hear a round of applause for our first competitor, Cheyenne Baker."

"There won't be as many riders tonight," Kit says as he hands me a beer.

"Why's that?"

"First night, there's anywhere from thirty to fifty, but only the top fifteen move on. And after tonight, the top eight will compete tomorrow."

"Damn, that's a lot of pressure. This is her first race since her injury, right?"

"Yeah." There's a thread of worry in his one-word answer, and the way he downs his beer tells me enough.

We fall silent as the first racer comes and goes. Kit takes notes on each rider. A peek shows me it's everything from their time to the angle of approach and body position.

"She's next."

My body tenses when Laramie and Xpresso burst through the open gate. I don't know anything about barrel racing outside what I gleaned last night and today, but something seems off. They're moving quickly but are far from the barrel on the first turn. Laramie shifts on X's back as dirt flies around her thundering hooves.

Next to me, Kit swears, then mutters, "She's in her head." He exhales when she goes around the second barrel, but when they bump the third, he's on his feet. "Shit."

The barrel tips and lands with an inaudible thud, but from the crowd's silence, you'd think it was a sonic boom.

"What happened?" I ask.

Kit's face twists into a grimace. "She just knocked herself out of the running for the purse."

When Kit and I get to the cool-down area, Laramie is already off Xpresso, her brown hair mixing with the horse's mane as she buries her face into X's neck. She stiffens when Kit puts a hand on hers. The one cradling her shoulder.

"Need help?" he asks.

She shrugs but doesn't meet either of our eyes. We silently follow her to X's stall, Laramie holding her shoulder the entire time.

I linger outside the stall door when we arrive, giving her some time with X and her dad. Kit hugs her, holding her like she's something fragile. Like she's his world.

My fingers curl against my thigh as I think of Tuesday and my dad. Have I ever once seen him comfort her? Hug her? Shit, I honestly can't think of a single time aside from a perfunctory arm around the shoulder for a photo op. What might our lives have been like if we'd been so lucky to be raised by a man like Kit Larson?

Kit plucks the hat off her head, hangs it on a nearby hook, and then kisses her hair. "I'm heading home tomorrow." His eyes lock on mine. "I don't know if I'll be able to make Pueblo."

Pueblo?

"S'okay," she mumbles. "Colorado is outside the drive zone." The smile tugging at her lips loosens the knot in the pit of my stomach. Seeing her bump her dad's hip with her own does even more, and the breath that weighed in my lungs finally escapes.

He whispers something in Laramie's ear then meets my gaze. A wordless conversation passes between us, the older man telling me to take care of his daughter. I nod, the movement solid and sure, and a plan forms in my mind.

Kit waves his goodbyes, and then it's just Laramie and me. And Xpresso, of course. "Tell me what to do." I shove my hands in my pockets and lean against the stall door.

The slight smile from earlier grows. "Well, you can start by actually coming into the stall."

"Ah, yes. I see." In two quick strides, I'm right next to her, gripping her hips, anchoring her to me.

There's the barest hint of a sniffle when she says, "I think a hug first, then we can move on to getting X brushed, watered, and fed."

I wrap my arms around her and bury my nose in her hair. She smells faintly of sweat, along with the usual sunshine, hay, and wildflowers: things I never knew I'd love mixed into a perfect bouquet that is uniquely her.

With a sigh, she breaks the hug. Her eyes dart between a shovel and a large bucket, but a glance at my tennis shoes has her laughing. Jerking her thumb at a bucket on the wall, she gives me instructions. "Fill that bucket with water; there's a spigot in the center of the walkway." She removes all the gear X wears, not even looking at me as she talks. "Xpresso isn't a fan of the Lubbock water, so I sweeten it a little to encourage her to drink. When you get back with the water, you can add that half bottle of apple juice in the corner to it."

Stepping up behind her, I brush her hair to the side and give her nape a kiss. "Yes, ma'am."

She shivers. "Such a good boy." My lips trace down the length of her neck until X snorts.

"I hear you, I hear you," I say to the horse, raising my hands. I snag the bucket and go to find the water. It's easy enough. There's a line of people waiting with buckets that look like mine. Everyone is friendly, chatting while they wait, and I soak in the atmosphere and opportunity to people-watch.

Finally, it's my turn, and I fill the bucket as instructed. I'm almost to the stall when a deep voice catches my attention. "Well, well, well, Lucky. Today just wasn't your day, was it?" There's an unmistakable sneer in his words.

"Why are you here, Cyrus?"

Quickening my steps, all my goodwill toward the rodeo community evaporates when the man—Cyrus—says, "Came to offer you another chance to ride something and actually get a prize."

I step into the stall as he grabs his cock through his jeans. *What the hell?*

My mouth opens, ready to tell this asshole to fuck off, but Laramie beats me to it.

"I told you the last time you made that disgusting offer, I don't ride Mini Shetlands. And even if I did, you couldn't pay me to touch you. Hell, the head of the NFR could walk up right now and promise me the title just to look at your nasty cock, and it'd be the easiest no ever."

My hands ball into fists when the cowboy rears back as if he's going to come after her, but then he spots my furious glare and shrugs. "Whatever. All you barrel bunnies are the same. Enjoy faking it for the prick, Lucky."

Laramie huffs out a brittle laugh. "Trust me, there's no faking where he's involved." Then her brown eyes harden. "Now, get out of my stall."

Every muscle in my body is taut, ready to forcibly remove this creep if he doesn't leave on his own, but he slinks away, muttering a few more insults over his shoulder.

"Who was that?" I ask, setting the bucket down and mixing in the apple juice.

"That was Cyrus McClain. The asshole X bit and part of the reason I ended up in PT." At my raised eyebrows, she waves. "Ninety percent my fault, but I'm putting the other ten on him. He baited me, and like a dummy, I fell for it, needing to prove myself."

"Does he always talk to you like that?" I can't stop the frown that pulls at my mouth.

"Yeah, but I can handle it."

Echoes of Tuesday and the creep at work who preyed on her and then tried to blackmail her flicker through my mind. "I'm sure you can, but what about someone who can't?"

She stops brushing X. "What do you mean?"

"I mean, not everyone is as brave as you, Trouble. Sometimes men like that... they take advantage of others, and the ones they hurt find themselves with no one on their side." I run my fingers through my hair. "Is there a governing board or someone you can report him to? That way, if anything else ever happens, there'll be a record of his behavior on file."

Laramie worries her lip between her teeth, deep in thought. "I never thought of that, to be honest. I always told him off, and he'd leave me alone for half a dozen events." She absently rubs her shoulder. "Shit, what if something happened because I didn't report him?"

"Hey." I move her hand away and lightly massage the area the way Dr. Panter did on my injury. "You aren't responsible for his actions." I swallow, the realization that what I said also applies to my father, Tuesday, and me. "And I'm not trying to mansplain or pressure you into doing anything."

Her chuckle is a balm. "Let me finish up with X, and then I'll go see the officials."

Before moving away from her, I ask, "Besides what just happened, how are you? I know your ride didn't go the way you planned."

"I'm okay." When I make a humming sound, she pauses and tilts her head as if reconsidering what she said. Slowly, she says, "I'm disappointed and embarrassed. I'm a better rider than what I showed today." Turning her beautiful face to mine, she whispers, "Knowing you were here, watching me, I got a little in my head."

Why would my being here make her nervous? Shit. Did I fuck up things for her?

"Uh, I'm sorry. I didn't—"

She stops me with her lips. I savor the pillowy softness of them, her lashes fluttering as she closes her eyes, her arms gliding around my neck. It doesn't matter that our mouths are locked together; I want her closer. Need her closer.

Hands roam, each of us clinging to the other, a thread of desperation mixing into the heat between us. Mine from the fear I cost her her comeback. Hers, from what I assume is the need to put her ride behind her.

It isn't until we hear an impatient stamp that we break apart. Laramie's lips are pink and swollen, and her cheeks are flushed. God, what I'd give to sink into her right now.

"Sorry, X. I'm not being a very good friend to you right

now, am I?" She soothes the horse, petting up and down her muzzle, slipping her a peppermint.

We manage to keep our hands off each other until Xpresso is settled. Our eyes meet, the tension between us growing thicker.

"Come to my trailer—"

"Come to my motel—"

We end up in my motel. Laramie ran by her trailer to clean up and pack a few items. While she was showering, I may have snooped, uncovering a velvet bag in one of the built-in drawers.

Do I regret rummaging through the stash of toys? Absolutely not. Did I pilfer a couple of items hoping to use them tonight? Hell yes.

Laramie drops into my lap, her lips brushing mine. "Told you those cheese sticks were Twinkie-sized."

The bed squeaks beneath us. "Always opening my eyes to the finer things in life, aren't you?"

"I'm trying to make up for your sadly deprived childhood."

She has no idea how accurate her words are. She's teasing me about food, but damn if that's not hitting the nail on the head.

Laramie reads the shift in my mood and cups my face. "Where'd you go?"

"Doesn't matter because I'm back now and exactly where I want to be."

Her eyes scan my face. "War, we can spend the night talking. You know that, right? I can be that person for you." She sucks in a deep breath then exhales. "The one you come to when you're hurting. When you need someone to take care of you."

My throat tightens, and in a flash, I flip us so Laramie lies on the bed beneath me. "What I need from you right now is this." I kiss her, deep and so hungry for more.

With gentle hands, I slip off her t-shirt. She's not wearing a bra, and I soak in the sight of her gorgeous tits. She fists my shirt, tugging on the hem.

Obliging her, I reach back and pull it over my head. The way her pupils dilate gives my ego a heady stroke.

"Lift those hips for me, sweetheart." I shimmy her leggings off, again treated to her lack of underwear. "Shit, Trouble. No bra, no panties. It's like you're begging to get fucked."

She smirks. "Maybe I am, Pretty Boy. Are you going to make me wait?"

Shucking my jeans and boxer briefs, I stroke my cock, enraptured by the sight of Laramie naked and wanting. I toss a condom on the bed then drape myself over her; the press of warm skin on skin has my eyes rolling back in my head. Laramie rises as much as she can, capturing me in a kiss, but I gently guide her shoulders into the mattress.

"I see you, Trouble. You want to buck me off and take the reins. The last time we did this, you were in charge, and I was *your* good boy. But that didn't work out for me the morning after."

She parts her mouth, but I settle my thumb on her lower lip, silencing whatever she's going to say.

"This time, I'm in charge."

Laramie nods, then kisses the pad of my thumb before biting. Not hard, but the nip and the fire in her brown eyes say she's willing to let me be in charge. For now.

I meet her gaze. "Hard limits?"

"No degradation."

"Anywhere I can't touch you?"

She writhes and lets out a whimper. "No."

"If you want me to stop for any reason—"

"I'll tell you. I promise."

With a smirk, I drag her arms above her head, crossing them at the wrist. "Keep these here. Understand?"

Her nose crinkles when she huffs.

"Laramie, answer me." I roll my hips, pressing my weight against the cradle of her pelvis. The gasp of air she sucks in tells me I'm hitting all the right spots.

"That feels good, doesn't it, sweetheart? I want to give you so much more, but I can't. Not until you promise you can follow *my* directions."

"Yes."

"So close. Yes what?"

She smiles, though it's more of a threat. "Yes, sir, I'll keep my arms above my head." Then, she adds, "For now."

I bark out a laugh and plunder her lips with mine. "I'll take it, Trouble."

My fingers walk her body. Anywhere I can touch, I do. Her hair, her ribs, her hips, her thighs. Meanwhile, my lips sweep along her jaw, then to the delicate pulse point in her neck. I can all but taste her heart picking up speed. My mouth travels lower, across her collarbone, before I grin into her sternum, my teeth snapping at the thin skin in the valley between her breasts. When her hands tangle in my hair, trying to guide my path, I snake a hand between our bodies and give her a quick spank right over her clit.

The resounding moan is music to my ears. "Keep those hands where I put them."

She smiles at me, a cheeky little thing. "I need another reminder, sir."

Topping from the bottom. Muffling my amusement, I ignore her request. "You'll get what I give you. Nothing more, nothing less." I shift my weight so she's more securely pinned beneath me. "It may be so many orgasms you beg for me to stop—your limbs shaking, your body exhausted in pleasure." She squirms, her hips and chest pressing upward, only to meet the wall of my body. With a dark chuckle, I continue. "Or it may be hours of teasing. Until you're so desperate, a warm breath on your pussy is enough to send you careening over the edge."

I suck on her nipple, worrying the nub until it pebbles against my tongue. "Tell me why you left."

She freezes beneath me.

I graze my teeth over her nipple, biting down when she stays silent. "Laramie, why did you leave?"

"I, um, I don't know."

Tsking, I rise from the bed. The weight of Laramie's eyes on me as I stride across the room.

"War?"

Not answering, I pull out the vibrating butt plug and lube.

Her eyebrows shoot up when she sees what I have. "Where did you... how did... what?"

"I found your secret stash while you were showering. Thought you might need some extra persuasion to answer questions."

"War, I'm sorry. I made a mis—"

"Shhh, sweetheart. I'm not mad. I just want answers. Honest ones. And this seems like the best way to get them while also wringing pleasure from you. Now, turn around."

I leave no room for argument, though I'd never make her do something she didn't want to. If she hesitates at all, this ends. But Laramie does as I command, twisting to her hands and knees, her ass and pink pussy on display for me.

"You're so gorgeous." I slide my cock between her lower lips, letting the head bump against her clit. While I tease her, I place a generous drop of lube in between her cheeks.

Her cute little asshole clenches, and she pushes into my touch. I start with one finger, teasing around her pucker. When she's taking it well, I add a second.

"You're doing so good. Such a good girl." I kiss up the line of her spine. Her entire body shudders and breaks out in goosebumps. I love that she's so responsive. I whisper more praises against her skin. Telling her how beautiful she is, how hard she makes me.

Then I slip my fingers out of her, relishing the gasp when I push the lubed plug in. I pull it out, add more lube, then work it in again.

"How's that feel?"

"So good," she moans.

I repeat that pattern until she's clawing at the sheets; only then do I push the plug in and leave it. "I'll be right back. Don't move." I climb off the bed and wash my hands before picking up the remote for the toy.

"Why did you leave that night, Trouble?"

A beat of silence.

Settling my forearm on her lower back so she can't move, I click the lowest setting and watch Laramie try to buck.

"Answer me."

"I w-was scared."

I reward her by pushing a finger into her pussy. "Keep going."

"You were, are, a distraction. God, War. More. Please."

A second finger joins the first, and I up the vibration pattern on the plug. "Did you plan to leave from the start?"

She drops her face into the mattress, muffling her answer. "Yes."

There's a heavy thread of sadness in that one word.

I shift so I can press my chest to her bare skin. "Thank you for being honest."

"But I went back."

"What?" My fingers still inside her.

She rocks against my hand, searching for friction and relief. "I went back. That morning. But you were already gone."

Is it possible for your heart to lurch? Because if so, mine just did. She came back to The Rusty Spur for me. Two fingers become three, and I kick the vibrations up as high as they go. "I believe you. Now be a good girl and come for me." My thumb works her clit until she's clenching my fingers.

Her release drenches my hand and sends another burst of pride through me. I did that. I made this strong, confident woman fall apart. "That's one. Next question. How did you know I sold my apartment?"

She groans. "I searched for you. Even asked Dr. Panter for your info. She wouldn't give it to me, but I figured out what building you lived in, and your doorman told me you were gone."

I curl my fingers, putting pressure on that spongy spot inside her as she answers. Between that, the vibrations, and the patterns I trace around her sensitive bud, she comes again.

"That's two. Last question." I pull my fingers from where they're buried and help her turn over. Making sure she's watching, I lick every bit of her honey off my hand; then I roll the condom down my length. Drawing a steadying breath, I ask the question I most need answered. "Do you want me?"

"Yes!"

"I don't mean my cock, Laramie. I mean me. All of me. For more than tonight."

Maybe it's flying too close to the sun, and this woman will always burn me, but I need her to say it.

I push my cock against her, hissing at the heat of her even through the thin latex. But I won't give her an inch, not yet. "Answer me, Laramie. Tell me this is more than tonight."

Her eyes are glassy when she cradles my cheek. "I want you. I want to date you, to know you, and to build something real with you."

Disbelief and a giddy sort of joy bubble through me, and like a thread pulled too tight, I snap, sinking my cock deep into her glorious warmth. "Listen to me, Trouble." I grit my teeth, the addition of the plug making her so damn tight. Not to mention the rumbly vibrations pulsing through that thin barrier inside her. "I'm head over heels for you. Have been since our first PT session, and it only grew with each conversation we had, each kiss. And that night we spent together..." I groan and kiss her hard before whispering against her lips. "But I'm about to fuck you like I hate you."

She mewls, and her pussy flutters around my cock. "Yes, god, yes."

I get to conquer her this time, but only because she lets me. I pull out, then drive in, setting a punishing pace. "Fuck, you're so wet and tight. So perfect."

Laramie claws at my back, her legs locking around my hips, holding me as close as possible. There's no finesse to my movements; it's simply desperate need.

"Yes, be a good girl and take it all. What I wouldn't give to be bare inside you."

"Next. Time." She pants between each word, lost in the rhythm between us.

"You're going to let me take this pussy raw? Let me fill you up?"

"I'm going to demand it." She nips my lip.

In between thrusts, I mutter against her mouth. *Thrust.* "So." *Thrust.* "Damn." *Thrust.* "Bratty."

She clenches around me, squeezing my cock, guiding me to my own blackout-worthy, blissful end.

"Need you to come. Right the fuck now."

"Yes, sir."

It's that snarky-sweet *sir* that pushes me over the edge. I grunt out my release, a tingle spreading from the base of my spine down to my balls. Laramie tumbles with me, crying out my name.

I roll us to our side, my cock still inside her. She's beautifully flushed, the light gleam of sweat on her skin.

Another mini orgasm rolls through her, and she whimpers. "War, the plug."

"Shit, sorry." I gently slide my cock out of her warmth and tie off the condom before scrambling for the remote and turning it off. Her sigh of relief as I ease the plug out of her has me fighting off a chuckle. Grabbing the used toy and condom, I toss one into the sink and the other into the trash, then get the water running.

Pink stains Laramie's cheeks as I bundle her into my arms and carry her to the bathroom. I settle her pliant form on the toilet and press a kiss to her forehead. "Do what you need, sweetheart, while the water warms up."

For probably the first time in her life, she doesn't argue. She's too blissed out to be bothered by my proximity, but I give her a semblance of privacy by turning my back and fiddling with the shower.

Once it's the perfect temperature, I guide her into the steady stream. She's unsteady on her feet and clings to me, which is no hardship on my part. I love that she's a quivering mess in my arms. I'm quick and efficient, washing all her overly sensitive parts. Leaving her carefully propped against the wall, I step out, tie a towel around my waist, then reach into the shower with another and wrap her up.

Like the precious cargo she is, I carry her to the bed. That she's letting me take care of her feeds something deep inside me, and I fall even harder for Laramie Larson.

After I get her tucked in, I click off the lights and climb in next to her. Her hand settles over my heart, and she taps my wrist. "What happened to your watch?"

"I left it on a table in a dive bar about thirty minutes before I showed up at the rodeo last night." I swallow. "I met my Dad for a drink. Some small part of me was hoping he would apologize. Realize that he's essentially pushed both his children out of his life. But it was more of the same, and that goddamn watch…"

"It's a symbol of the world you left behind," Laramie whispers.

"And a gift from him. A physical cuff shackling me to him, and I wanted it gone."

She picks up my hand and kisses the inside of my wrist. "Do you feel lighter?"

I shrug. "I haven't really thought about it, but I do."

"Then you made the right choice."

A quiet yawn slips from her lips, and her body softens against mine. Another minute passes before her breathing slows. I muffle a groan when she snuggles her tight ass closer.

"You asleep, Trouble?" She mumbles something and buries her cheek into the cheap cotton pillowcase but otherwise doesn't stir.

Lowering my voice so it's barely audible over the creaky ice machine outside the room, I whisper my secrets while playing with the strands of Laramie's hair. "You're amazing. You know that? A creature of instinct and wild and wind. Some sort of earth-born goddess who crashed into my life just as I shattered the only world I've known. Finding you here is a sign from the universe. Proof I did the right thing, for once. I don't deserve you, but if my time with Tuesday has taught me nothing else, it's that life and family are what you make it. And I want the chance for you to be both. My life and my family."

Closing my eyes, I drift off to restful sleep, confident in the knowledge I'll wake with Laramie in my arms in the morning.

CHAPTER THIRTEEN
Laramie

I wake to the warm press of a naked body against my back and the firm grip of a large hand on my boob. *War.* Grinning in the still-dark room, I disentangle myself from his arms and pad into the bathroom.

Clicking the door closed behind me, I take care of business, then stop and check myself out. My hair is a sex-swept mess, and pink mouth-shaped bruises mark the column of my neck. Darker smudges—fingerprints—decorate my hips. I look well-fucked and well-loved.

Pink warms my cheeks as I think about what went on between us. I'm not usually one to give up control in the bedroom, but ceding to War was freeing. Being in the moment, focusing on every ounce of pleasure he wrested from my body. It's something I'll do over and over with him. For him.

While his bossy side was incredibly sexy, what drove it was even more so. Beneath the physical was the need for me to affirm that this thing between us is real—that I want him for more than a night. *And, god, I do.*

Shame spasms in my stomach. I royally fucked up when I

left him at The Rusty Spur. Good thing the universe granted me a second chance to show him how sorry I am.

"Laramie?" There's a thread of unease in War's voice as it sounds outside the closed door. Can't have that. Swinging it open, I jump into his arms, catching him off-guard. He lets out an *oomph* and attempts to keep us upright but fails, and we crash to the bed, flopping like a pair of decked fish.

Through a series of twists, rolls, and giggles, we end up with me sitting astride him, my legs splayed on either side of his hips.

With a quick swoop, I plant a kiss on his lips. "Morning, Pretty Boy."

He tucks a strand of hair behind my ear then brushes his knuckles up and down my cheek. "You stayed."

"I promised I would." A raw ache pinches in my chest. I hate that those are his first words to me this morning, but it's another reminder of how much I hurt him. I cradle the hand still resting against my cheek, bringing it to my lips and kissing the center of his palm.

War's cock kicks to life beneath me, his body's physical response to my touch. When I grind my bare pussy down on his lap, his eyes flutter, and he lets out a needy moan. "Last night was—shit, I'm not sure I have the vocabulary to describe it."

"I think the word you're looking for is fan-fucking-tastic." At his rough laugh, I grin and toss my hair. "You did a decent job being in charge, Pretty Boy, but I can't wait for it to be my turn to show you how it's done."

He smirks and bucks his hips, the hard line of his cock rocking against me. "I think the four orgasms I wrecked you with were more than decent."

"Three and a half; the last one was a residual effect from the toy."

"You're going to put me in an early grave with all this bickering."

I snort and glide my pussy up and down his length, loving the way it jerks against me as if it has a mind of its own. "You love it."

War's hands grip me so I can't wiggle. All the playfulness melts from his features. His lips press into a firm line, and his honey gaze sears me. "I do."

It's only two words, but their weight knocks the air from my lungs. Before I can think, let alone respond, he pulls me flush to his chest and captures my lips. His tongue takes advantage of my shock to swirl with mine, and he palms my ass. I'm pressed against him and let the power of his touch roll over me.

When he moans, I snap back to my senses, giving as good as I get, sucking on his tongue, tracing inside his lips. I'm practically pulsating for him, ready to demand he fuck me when he eases up, switching to chaste pecks at the corners of my mouth and along my jaw.

"You have no idea what you do to me, Trouble." Our mouths are so close that each word is a puff against my lips. We stay that way, each of us breathing the other's air, heady waves of something far more substantial than *like* crashing over me.

War nuzzles his nose against mine. "Come to Trail Creek with me."

I swear my eyebrows jump to my hairline, and I sit up, scouring his face for any hint he's teasing. A thousand reasonable reasons to say no run through my head. It's too soon. The guys I dated in the past couldn't handle my independence. I travel over half the year.

But then I think of last night. How right it feels to be with War. "Are you serious?"

"Laramie, I just got you back. I want to be where you are, or I want you where I am. And since you won't be staying here..." He glances at me as if worried his reminder of my failed ride will derail the conversation.

"Go on," I whisper.

"I don't know how long you have until Pueblo, but I looked, and it's about three and a half hours from Trail Creek."

It's not that I don't want to go. I do. Every fiber of my being wants more time with him. A chance to see where he's living now, find out more about what happened after I left Dallas, explore his skin with my tongue. And my twin devils are cheering me on, hollering for me to sprint head first down this hill that leads to War. But... "Is there somewhere I could board X?" Not even my shoulder demons—or desire for this man—can override the sense of responsibility I have for my girl.

"I'm not sure..." He frowns, deep in thought. "I can ask Tuesday. Between her friends, they know everyone in town. If there's a place that boards large animals, one of them will know."

"And you want me to meet her? Your sister?" I hold my breath, waiting for his reply.

"Yes." His quick answer culls my doubts. "You'll like her, and she'll love you, especially when she hears you put me in my place once or twice." He swallows. "Tuesday and I... I told you we weren't close for a long time, that I made so many mistakes. Wasn't who she needed."

My hands glide over his chest, seeking to calm the anguish in his words.

"We started talking more after the showdown with *Mr. Phillips*, but picking up and going to New Mexico changed everything. For the first time in my life, she and I were together without the toxic influence and expectations of our parents." He chuckles and scrubs his hand over his beard. "Granted, I wasn't in the best place, but she took me in like I was dumb for asking. She built this whole family and life." There's a thread of wistfulness in his words. "And invited me to be a part of it even though I didn't deserve it."

Before I can assure him he deserves all that and more, my phone goes off. Reaching over him, I snag it off the small end table. Instead of sitting back up or getting off his lap, I stretch out, treating him like my personal man pillow.

> **DADDIO**
>
> Mornin' Mimi. I've got to get back. Want me to take X, your truck, and the trailer? Think you can make it here by 9:00 to get some clothes?

I read his text twice, wondering if the fog of the amazing sex I had last night, the high of War asking me to meet his sister, and the disappointment of not placing have short-circuited my brain.

"What's wrong?" War asks.

"My dad..."

He sits up, taking me with him, cradling me in his lap. "Is he hurt?"

I shake my head. "No. Nothing like that. He's offering to take X home."

A brilliant smile breaks out over War's face. "Well, that solves the boarding problem, doesn't it?"

"I guess so, but how would he... Why would he..." My words falter, trying to figure out what's driving my dad to offer this. "I haul X. Dad can't make it to all my rodeos; some are multi-day drives. Even when it's somewhat close, like this one, he rents a car and follows me up. It's weird."

"Weird, but fortuitous." He hugs me. "There's no reason for you not to come to Trail Creek now. Unless you don't want to." There's a myriad of emotions in his voice, from happy to anxious. He forces the next words out. "Which is okay. I'd understand."

Maybe it's all chance; maybe it's fate. Either way, I don't care. This is the gift of time, and I want time with War Phillips. To know him, to learn life with him, to love him. And right now, that means going to Trail Creek and meeting his family.

I smooth the frown from between his eyebrows with my thumb then kiss him in the same spot. "Come on, Pretty Boy, let's go get my clothes." The way his face lights up is something I'll cling to for the rest of my days.

As he goes to move, I fixate on the flex of his pecs from under the dusting of chest hair. His stomach is softer than when we first met, but I like it—a lot. Biting my bottom lip, I give him a heated glance. "My dad is leaving in just under an hour. We're fourteen minutes from the arena."

War raises an eyebrow, waiting for me to go on.

"How many times do you think you can make me come in thirty-seven minutes?"

In a flash, I'm staring up at War's handsome face, his weight pressing me into the mattress. "Let's find out."

Turns out the answer is four. I think taunting him about it *only* being three and a half last night made him more determined. War and my toys work *very* well together. When he busted out the magic wand, I was done for. It's taken a shared shower—where I was little more than a posable figure—and twelve of the fourteen minutes of the drive for me to recover.

War smacks of masculine superiority, having brought me to begging at one point during our morning romp. If I wasn't so blissed out, I might be annoyed. As it stands, I'm just satisfied and swoony.

When we near the rodeo grounds, I direct him toward a different entrance so he can go into the trailer hold.

"It's bizarre that so many people travel and live this way." He says it absently, almost to himself.

"It's not for the weak of heart."

His brown eyes meet mine, chagrin coloring his features. "I didn't mean to be rude."

"You may have relaxed some." I wave my hand at his hair, beard, and clothes. "But deep in your heart, you're a Dallas city boy. This must seem like a whole other planet to you. No posh dining or luxury high-rise apartments or sprawling McMansions." I scoot as close as my seat allows and walk my fingers up his thigh. "Plus, I remember how shocked you were when I took you to Stir-ups and The Rusty Spur."

A rosy hue creeps over his cheeks. "I was a snob, and you proved all my doubts wrong."

An unhappy humming sound claws its way from my throat. "You left the clothes behind."

The car jerks to a stop, and I find my seatbelt unbuckled and myself hauled into his lap. It's a tight fit, and my ass presses into the steering wheel.

"I did." He brings our foreheads together. "I couldn't take them. It was too raw that morning. I couldn't walk out of there with a physical reminder."

Another suffocating swell of guilt smashes into me. Pretty words rest on the tip of my tongue, eager to slip free of their confines and soothe him. But for what's likely only the third time in my life, I think before I speak. I search my heart for any hint of a lie, and, when I find nothing, I embrace the warm glow lighting me from the inside. Losing last night led me to be here with him this morning, and while I'm not looking to hang up my Stetson anytime soon, the future I picture looks vastly different than I imagined it even forty-eight hours ago. With complete and total sincerity, I grip his hair, anchoring myself to him.

"We're going to find a way to put that night behind us. I don't mean forget it. It will always be a part of our story, but I will prove it to you, however you need. Show you how much I regret leaving you. I'm in, War. All in. There's nowhere else I want to be."

His grasp on me tightens, and he buries his face in the crook of my neck. The warmth of his breath mixes with the heat of his lips as they ghost along my throat. "Laramie, I—"

A rap on the driver's side window pulls us apart, and I groan when I meet my father's amused stare. Shooing him away from the door, I pop it open and tumble out.

"Looks like you two were having a moment."

I roll my eyes and hip-check him. "We were until someone interrupted us."

Dad hugs me tight. "You two look good together."

Craning my head back, I ask, "Why did you offer to drive the truck?"

He shrugs. "Thought you might want to take advantage of having a few bonus days off, and no offense to the Boss, but she can be a little high maintenance." I grin. He's not wrong. I love Xpresso, but she's a diva. Dad steps back and jerks his head toward the trailer. "Pack up what you think you might need."

"I'll go get her majesty from her stall."

"I already paid one of the local hands to get her ready." My mouth drops, and I'm about to argue that he shouldn't have done that when he gives me his *remember that time you stole my truck* look. "You listen to me, Laramie Louise Larson."

I glance at War to see if he heard Dad middle-name me,

and from the smile he's struggling to contain, the obvious answer is yes.

"You take these next four days and get to know War. Enjoy the time in New Mexico. I've got X, and I'll make sure she's in Pueblo in plenty of time for the Cimmaron Classic."

I'm about to say my goodbyes when it hits me. "Hold up!" I look between Dad and War. "How did you know I'm going to New Mexico?"

Two muscular arms wrap around me. "I told him."

"When? How?"

War smiles and whispers so only I can hear him. "Remember after orgasm three when you squirted all over me and demanded I go get a towel?" At my slight nod, he goes on. "I also fired off a text to your dad. You were so out of it you didn't even notice me using your face to unlock your phone."

I'm torn between impressed and irked. But when War's lips brush my nape, impressed wins. I give Dad one last hug and a wave before climbing into the trailer and packing for my next adventure.

The drive to Trail Creek is enlightening. War is a fan of sports talk radio from one specific Dallas station, which he plays through an app on his phone. He's also a gas station snob, which isn't surprising. I do talk him into stopping at an Allsup's and splitting a fried burrito once during the six-hour car ride. He declines my offer to drive but agrees to play twenty questions, the license plate game, and one very disturbing game of Would You Rather.

It's early evening when we arrive in Trail Creek. The small

town is adorable, like something from a movie set. I've been to my fair share of small towns, and they come in all shakes and shapes. But this place is a real gem.

I giggle as I read the business names, noting all the places I want him to take me while I'm here. As if reading my mind, War says, "The Bee and The Bean has a delicious pecan coffee blend, and their pastries are amazing."

"Yeah?"

"Yeah. Tuesday's future sister-in-law, Clairy, owns it. She took over for her aunt not too long ago."

"I spotted the bookstore."

War snorts. "Oh yeah, we'll have to make a stop, or Saul will hunt us down."

"Who's Saul?"

"He's like the self-proclaimed Trail Creek czar." At my arched brow, he smiles. "He's a nice guy, just intense. Very interested in who's coming and going. And apparently, he keeps all the town's activities alive."

Twisting so I can see him better, I pepper him with questions. "Tell me more. What else does this little town have going on? Any other big-wigs I should be aware of?"

"There's this eclectic vegetarian food truck. The menu rotates almost weekly based on whatever the owner wants to make. A kick-ass staple restaurant, Ava's—you have to try her stuffed sopapillas. And there's no way Tuesday will let you leave before you've had a Flocked Up Flamingo at her friend Dane's bar."

"I'm afraid to ask."

His chuckle is quickly becoming one of my favorite sounds. "They're better kept a surprise."

"Does your sister know we're here?"

"Yeah, she's been texting me, demanding location updates

for the past thirty minutes. I wouldn't be surprised if there's a welcome committee waiting at the house I'm renting."

Sure enough, when we pull up to a small A-frame cabin, three cars idle in the driveway. War shoots me a reassuring smile before narrowing his eyes at my door. "Wait there. I'm coming around to open it."

I roll my eyes but do as he says. A small part of me might be a touch worried about meeting War's people. The idea of walking up to them with his hand laced in mine helps ease the nerves.

By the time we get to the covered front porch, a group of six waits. They're clearly friends, all chatting together. There's a tall, striking woman with loose waves and a full sleeve of tattoos laughing next to a handsome man with a frown on his face. A giant man with shoulder-length blond hair and a matching beard towers over them both. His paw of a hand rests on the hip of a woman an inch or two shorter than me, with curves for days. And closest to us stands a grinning couple. The man has on a baseball cap, his dark brown curls peeking out from beneath the brim. He has the most piercing blue eyes I've ever seen. Standing with her back to his chest is a woman, again slightly shorter than me, with hair that reminds me of a sunset. She's beautiful, and despite this being my first time seeing her, I know exactly who she is. The eyes. They are a gorgeous, warm honey brown, just like her brother's.

CHAPTER FOURTEEN

war

Trail Creek, New Mexico
March

Tuesday rushes forward to hug me and then Laramie. I offer my hand to Bond, keeping my eyes on my sister and the woman I'm falling for. It's no surprise to find the Davis sisters and their respective not-boyfriends here alongside Tuesday and Bond. The Davises are a close-knit group.

As much as I appreciate them being here, I'm also itching to get Laramie into my bed to spend hours learning everything she likes. It's not that I haven't made the most of our time together, but the days ahead are a gift I have to take advantage of.

What happens when it's time for her to go to Pueblo? Maybe I'll go with her. If she wants me to... Shit, maybe I should have thought beyond this week.

Laramie hugs me from behind. "Hey, you okay?"

I squeeze her forearms. "Yeah, just thinking."

"That's dangerous," Tuesday says, a smile on her lips. It

falters when she meets my gaze, but she fixes it back in place and I'm reminded of the Tuesday from before. The one who lived under a microscope and wore that fake, placating smile more days than I can count.

"I don't want to add to whatever's got you so deep in thought, but this came for you while you were in Lubbock." Bond holds out a small box. I recognize the pricy wrapping paper and my father's wax emblem sealing it shut.

Tuesday eyes the box like it might be a bomb. "It showed up at the Davis Designs office yesterday afternoon. The note said your name. Nothing else."

Swallowing, I push down the uncertainty of what comes after Laramie's next rodeo. Stuff it deeper, alongside the worry that niggles in my gut about the box. Lock it all in an iron cage with the fear of starting life over in my thirties.

I blink and shake my head, lighter with those concerns trapped for now. I lean down and flutter my lips across Laramie's; then I turn to my friends and sister. "Thanks for coming out to meet us. Everyone, this is Laramie. Laramie, this is everyone."

Like the ball-busting angel she is, Laramie says, "I'm sure War meant to give me your names, but after the long drive, he knows I'm exhausted. He raved about The Bee and The Bean. Any chance I could see you guys there tomorrow and properly introduce myself? You know, not dressed in road clothes." She gestures to her yoga pants and a threadbare t-shirt that says *I raise plants, animals, and eyebrows in 4H.*

"Of course! We'll meet you there at eight for breakfast. Does that work?" Tuesday asks.

Laramie nods and hugs my sister, whispering something in her ear that has Tuesday smiling. Those two are going to be double trouble for sure. Add Charli and Clairy into the mix, and they'll be town-wide menaces.

I wait on the porch, talking with Bond a few minutes more after opening the front door and encouraging Laramie to poke around inside. I figure it's payback for snooping through her toy drawer.

"So that box..." Bond says.

"Yeah. It's from our dad."

"Figured. Tuesday's been glaring at it ever since it showed up." My future brother-in-law pats me on the shoulder. "I don't know everything that went down while you guys were growing up. Tuesday's told me bits and pieces, and I've seen how far you two've come in the last three months. I still don't know what caused you to step up in December, but men like Warren Phillips don't take an L lightly."

"Oh, that I know," I say with a shrug. "It doesn't matter what's in there. It could be the keys to Phillips Construction, and I still wouldn't have anything to say to him."

"Just be sure, man. Tuesday wants you here. Or at least somewhere you can be happy." He cants his head toward my living room, where Laramie bounces on each couch cushion.

My hand comes up to the back of my head. "She's a nomad. A rolling stone. Chasing her fortune on the back of a horse at forty miles an hour."

"But does she make you happy?"

I don't need to think. "Yeah. She's amazing, and I'd tether myself to her forever, but..." I sigh. "I don't want to drag her down."

Bond swings an arm around my shoulder. "Then you find a way to run alongside her."

Once Bond and Tuesday leave, I shut the door and drop onto the couch next to Laramie. She climbs into my lap, burying her nose in the hollow of my throat.

"Want to talk about it?" she asks, her words muffled.

"Not tonight, but soon." My head drops, resting against the

couch. "Right now, I want to shower with you to get the road off us; then, I want to take you to bed."

"Hmm, luckily for you, that's exactly what I want, too."

Laramie climbs out of my lap and saunters off like she owns the place. I sit slack-jawed, watching her navigate my rental like she's been here for months, not twenty minutes.

Over her shoulder, she calls, "I took your permission to explore and ran with it."

Why doesn't that surprise me?

A minute later, I hear the rush of water and her voice. "Are you joining me or not, Pretty Boy?"

My cock twitches, and I beeline to the beautiful woman waiting for me. She's already under the steady stream, her hands running up and down her body. As if she can feel the weight of my gaze, she cranes her head and winks before bending—giving me a perfect peak at her pink pussy—and snagging my body wash. When she straightens and turns, my eyes latch onto the drops that land on her chest.

Never looking away, she brushes one soapy hand over her skin, her fingers tracing circles along the sides of her body. Her fingers drop lower, leaving a haphazard trail of my scent across her stomach and hips.

"It's getting awful lonely in here."

I shed my clothes and slip into the warm water behind her. *Fuck.* There's nothing like the feeling of Laramie's wet, supple body against mine. My hands roam her curves, feather-light touches across her hips, her shoulders, down the length of her arms. She melts into me and moans.

"That noise is nothing but trouble, just like you." I suck on her earlobe and buck my hips.

Laramie reaches between us and glides her hand up and down my cock. Her firm grip pulls a hiss from between my clenched teeth as I fight not to fuck her fist.

"Let me take care of you first, sweetheart."

She pouts but drops her hand. I step back and pick up my shampoo, then take a beat to drink her in. Her long lashes are damp from the mist of the shower, and her hair curls around her face. She's a goddess.

Her eyes slip closed as I work my fingers through her hair, and she makes another of those delicious noises. I want to cover her mouth with mine and sip those moans like a fine wine.

I tip her head back and rinse the suds from her hair. She's bathed in my scent, and I want nothing more than to add my cum to the mix. Marking her inside and out.

Laramie turns the full power of her attention on me. "Now, let *me* take care of *you*."

She kisses a trail along my chest while her soapy hands massage my back, glutes, and thighs, summoning a series of shivers that wrack my body.

A groan rips from my throat when she sinks to her knees on the tile before me. Laramie toys with me, kissing my inner thighs, grazing her teeth along the sensitive skin. The more she teases me, the more I jerk and moan. She takes me into her mouth, running her tongue along the underside of my shaft, pressing against the sensitive vein that runs the length of it.

"Shit, Trouble." One of my hands drops to her head, petting the wet strands in a mix of needing to touch her and needing to see her.

As if the extra weight of my hand urges her on, she takes me to the back of her throat and swallows around me. What are words? Mine have all fled, and only inarticulate noises remain.

Her whimpers vibrate around me, harmonizing with mine, and together we write a wordless symphony.

My body is no longer mine to control; it's beholden to her.

When she digs her fingers into my ass, urging me deeper, I have to comply. Hips thrusting, cock aching, I'm desperate for the heat of her mouth.

But this isn't how I want to come, and certainly not before my girl. With a pained moan, I pull back, slipping free from Laramie's mouth. There's a thin string of spit still tethering my cock to her lips, and it takes all my willpower to keep from sinking deep into her throat and feeding her my cum.

"Bed." It's a grunt and all I can manage. Luckily, Laramie doesn't need more.

We're a flurry of teeth, lips, and hands as we bump our way from the shower to my bedroom. There's no drying off, no stopping for towels, only hunger.

The only thing stopping me from sinking into her as soon as her back hits my mattress is that I don't have a condom. "Shit." I rise, stretching for my nightstand, but a small hand on my bicep stops me.

"I told you. Next time, I wanted you with nothing in between us. I had a full STI panel run as part of my workup after you and I slept together in December. It came back negative." She chews on her plump bottom lip. "There hasn't been anyone since, and I have an implant."

"You're going to make me lose it, saying shit like that, Trouble." I run my nose down the column of her throat and nip at the sensitive juncture where her neck meets her shoulder. Murmuring into her skin, I say, "I've never gone without a condom and last tested in November as part of my regular physical. I haven't been with anyone since you either."

The admission that neither of us found comfort from another partner during our time apart acts like a trigger, and our mouths crash together. It's bruising, biting, rough, and raw. It's clashing teeth, sharp nips, and soothing kisses.

I break away, ready to lick my way down her body, when

Laramie uses the considerable strength in her thighs to roll us, and much like our first night together, I find myself beneath her.

"If you wanted to be on top, sweetheart, you could have asked."

"Not asking tonight, War. It's my turn, and I need you to be a very good boy for me." She licks her lips and smiles. "Is my throne ready?"

My eyebrows draw together. Her throne? It hits me as she begins a slow shift from my hips to my lower stomach and then higher. *Her throne.*

I pat my lips. "Hell yes, Trouble. Get that pretty pussy up here and drown me in your honey."

Kneeling above me, Laramie straddles my face, leaving me with a wide-open view of all her glory. Every bit of her, from her neatly trimmed patch of dark curls, to her clit peeking out from between her pink pussy lips, all the way to both her holes.

Heat radiates from her core, and I dive in, proffering myself to the magnificent creature above me. Laramie needs no guidance or encouragement as she fucks herself against my mouth and uses my nose to tease her clit.

My tongue delves into her pussy, fucking in and out of her before I suck one of her lips between mine. I savor the taste of her, that uniquely *Laramie* flavor.

She moans and circles her hips as she rides my face, praise raining down on me along with her desire. "You're doing so good. Making such a mess of me."

She's right. It's sloppy and wet and perfect.

"God, War, I'm going to come. I'm so close. Please, Pretty Boy, be so good for me and make me come with your tongue."

Her appreciation nurtures some of the broken parts of me—the parts I lock away to avoid. It smooths out some of the rough edges so those jagged bits are no longer stabbing me from the inside.

"Yes!" Laramie cries out as she loses herself in the throes of her climax. With one last whimper, she crumples onto the bed next to me, her chest rising and falling as she pants.

I can't resist turning my face to the toned thigh next to my head and running my lips along her skin. "Feel good, sweetheart?"

She doesn't answer, just sits up with a lascivious grin. I blink and Laramie is astride me like I'm her personal pony. Holding the base of my cock, she takes my entire length in one downward thrust.

We let out matching groans as I fill her to the brim. Being bare inside her is like nothing I can describe. It's silk and heat and pressure, and I never want to leave.

Despite the fast start, Laramie sets a slow, sensual pace. Her hips circle and rock, and she guides my hands to her tits. I lose myself in her. The heat of her pussy, the clench of her muscles around my cock, the weight of her palm-sized breasts, and the pebbled tips of her nipples.

She picks up the tempo, riding me harder, faster. "Come for me, War. Fill my pussy up. I want to feel you. Hot and thick inside me."

The dirty words spur me onward, the two of us sprinting toward our ends. Her face twists into a mask of ecstasy, and her inner muscles clamp around me. Despite wishing I could make this last longer, the tight flutters of her walls drag me over the edge, and I spend myself inside her.

I pull her to me and kiss all over her face, peppering her chin, lips, cheeks, and forehead. Our hearts thunder in concert, matching beat for beat. She smells like sex and my body wash. It feeds a possessive need I didn't know I had. She's mine. In this moment—and if I have my way, forever—she's mine.

The past four days have been the best of my life. Each morning, I wake up with Laramie in my arms, her soft body pressed against mine. She's charmed everyone she's met, even Saul. Living here permanently isn't in the cards for her—or me, to be honest. She's got too much invested in her barrel racing career and her dad's horse breeding business. Still, it's nice to know we'd always be welcome.

Today, I'm up before the sun, thanks to a brain that won't stop spinning. Tomorrow, she leaves for Pueblo, the next stop on the circuit, and I don't know where that leaves us. I haven't worked up the nerve to invite myself along, and Laramie hasn't offered.

There's no indication she's scared or rethinking us, but part of me is waiting for the other shoe to drop. It's not about her leaving me back in Dallas; it's about her not giving up her dreams and me not knowing what mine are—outside of her.

I was serious when I told Bond I don't want to drag her down. I did it to Tuesday for almost thirty-four years. She shines now. Free and happy. Her new light comes from being out from under my parents' thumbs, sure, but I can't help but think it also comes from being away from me.

Next to me, Laramie snuggles closer. She's been the big spoon all night, one arm thrown around my waist, the other tucked under her cheek. In charge, even in her sleep.

Careful not to wake her, I slip out from her hold and stifle a laugh when she frowns and tugs a pillow into her clutches. I rummage through my dresser and slip into a pair of sweats before padding down the hall and into the living room.

The box Tuesday and Bond brought with them the night

we arrived in town sits on the bar that separates this room from the kitchen. I grab it, tossing it from hand to hand, debating whether to open it now, later, or bury it in the backyard. Sighing, I wander back to the couch and drop onto the springy cushions. Treating the box like a basketball, I shoot it up and catch it until it's snatched out of the air.

"I've given you four days of wait time, Pretty Boy. You ready to talk about this?" At my nod, she plops down next to me. "It's from your dad?" Again, I nod. Laramie shakes the box, holding it to her ear as if that will release all its secrets. "I'm not trying to overstep, but if you want to open it, I'll hold your hand."

Pulling her closer, I kiss her hair and tangle my fingers with hers. Laramie's hands are rough, working hands. Hands that have grown up holding reins and pulling her back up when she falls. That she's here now, offering those hands to me... God, I'm gone for this woman.

Laramie looks at me, waiting for my confirmation. When I sharply jerk my head up and down, she pulls on the expensive ribbon and pops the folded seams. "I made the first tear. Your turn."

Somehow, it's less daunting, seeing the ribbon—that probably took my mother hours of her life to decide on—crumpled on the floor and the heavy-weight paper torn. I hook a finger into the rip and pull. As the rest of the wrapping falls away, I'm left with a velvet box.

I know what this is.

I snap open the lid, and there lies my watch. The one I left on a table with my dad in a dive bar in Lubbock. There's a small folded card below the timepiece.

> Warren -
> Consider this my final offer: You will return to Dallas and Phillips Construction as a one-third owner. Out of my

generosity, I will restore your sister to a silent one-third owner, though she will remain in New Mexico except for pre-agreed-upon company and family events. Neither of you deserves this, but I am offering it despite your repeated disappointments.

If I do not receive a response from you and Tuesday by the end of the month, I will take your silence as agreement to fully disinherit you both. At that point, there will be no further communication between us. You will cease to exist in this family.

Think long and hard about the consequences of your actions. How much your mother and I have done for you both. I have been more than patient. Your selfish and childish behavior has embarrassed this family and tarnished its name. It is time for you to grow up and take responsibility. Prove to me you are capable of salvaging what respect remains.

- Warren Phillips Sr.

My temper flares, and I crush the note and drop the box holding the watch to the ground. Everything around me fades as I stomp on the timepiece over and over. Five times. Ten times. So many times, I lose count.

"War." The sound of my name is a pebble in the ocean.

Every hurt. Every slight. Every time I changed myself to be what he expected. Every dream I let go to please him. I smash it all.

There's movement near me, a faint blur in my peripheral, but I am too lost in my rage to pay it mind. I don't feel the glass shattering and splintering beneath my bare foot. Or the red gold frame warping and denting. I don't even notice the traces of blood on the floor. It's not until Laramie shoves me to the couch and barks out a command that I'm jolted back to reality.

"War! Stop it! You're hurting yourself."

She's on her knees before me, this time for a totally different reason, her lips pressed into a firm line. There's a washcloth in her hand, and she narrows a harrowing glare my way. "Give me your feet."

"No, you don't need to—"

"Now." The fierceness in that single word stops me from any future protests.

Laramie cradles my foot like I'm a delicate bird and dabs at the cuts before pulling out a first aid kit and a slim pair of tweezers. She stops working long enough to hand me my phone. "Call your sister."

I take my phone, walk on shredded feet to the kitchen, and pour myself a generous shot of bourbon. Downing it, then another, I hobble back to the couch and collapse next to Laramie, my head buried in my hands.

What the actual fuck? Anger and disgust roil in my gut. Whatever small sliver of a ledge I stood on when considering going back to Dallas is demolished. Blown apart by two dollars' worth of linen and ink.

Ten minutes later, Tuesday and Bond crash through my front door. The mess I made—at least the physical one—is gone. Swept away with warm water and a broom. If only I could say the same about the emotional destruction left in its wake.

CHAPTER FIFTEEN

laramie

I rarely wish ill on people. Karma and all that. But Warren Phillips *Sr.*—as he so warmly signed the card to his son—is someone I wish a lifetime of tooth loss and irreversible genital shrinkage on.

I've always known how lucky I am to have my dad, but reading that note... Some people shouldn't be parents.

> **DADDIO**
> Game plan?

I glance at War, but his eyes are closed, so I text with one hand and stroke his head with the other.

> Unsure. Some crap went down with War's dad.
>
> That man is a piece of shit. Makes me want to take Biscuit from him.

> I don't think he's exactly hands on with his horse.
>
> Anything I can do?

> Nope. I'm gonna ask War to come to Pueblo and maybe on to Denver. I don't know if he's interested, and that's a lot of time together with someone I just met.

I chew on the inside of my cheek and wonder what Dad will think of what I say next.

> I'm falling hard, and I'm not ready to let him go.

> Then you know what you should do. Be smart, be safe, Mimi. But also be brave.

Smiling at Dad's last bit of advice, I scoot closer to War and tuck his face into my neck. He's been quiet since he hung up with Tuesday, only apologizing to me for losing his cool and making a mess—as if the random springs and gears were my concern.

I dig my fingers into his hair, rubbing his scalp and nape. I put light pressure on the shoulder he was rehabbing, and he lets out a muffled moan.

Keeping his face buried, he says, "You deserve better than me."

Strike two-hundred and forty-seven Warren Phillips Sr.

I slip my thumb under War's chin and guide his face to mine. My lips skate over his mouth, cheeks, and eyes until I rest my forehead against his. "How about you let me decide what I deserve?"

This earns me a smirk and a kiss before those burdens he's carried for so long weigh his mouth down to a flat line. The scent of honeyed bourbon lingers on his breath, and anger, resentment, and sadness ooze from him. He pulls away, slouching into the couch cushions.

I don't push, just go back to carding my fingers through his hair and waiting. I take advantage of his eyes being shut to study him. Each day we've been here, he's trimmed his beard a little more. Now, it's neat and short, highlighting his handsome features. I'm torn on which version of War is the most handsome. Business War with short hair and a clean-shaven face? Rugged War with long hair and an overgrown beard? Or this new version of War, Laramie's War, who's a mixture of both. Yes, this one is my favorite.

An annoyed huff rumbles through me. He thinks I deserve better than him? This man who saw that what he was doing was wrong and worked to make it right with his sister. Turned down money and what most would call an ideal life because once those blinders were off, he could never go back. Walked away from his toxic parents, job, and hometown to start fresh.

Say what you will, but change like that takes real determination and grit.

Did he make mistakes? Yes. If I were Tuesday, would I want to stuff a sea salt croissant up his nose? Also yes. But I have no doubts about who this man is and will be.

And I want him for more than these four days.

A rush of nerves floods my system, sending too much adrenaline to my heart. It's pounding so loud he has to hear it. Asking him to go with me is a huge risk. What would he do while I compete? A man like War needs purpose. What if I can't ride with him there? My track record knowing he's in the audience is oh-for-one. And he definitely didn't seem impressed by the nomadic lifestyle I lead. How would he survive when I hitch my house to my truck and haul it to the next town?

I roll my lips to stop the giggle trying to escape when I think of how he'd react to some of the rest stops I visit on the road.

But these past four days have been game-changers. I worried being in such close proximity would overwhelm me.

That we'd bicker or annoy each other to the point that when Pueblo came around, he'd be pushing me out the door. It certainly wouldn't be the first time a guy dropped me as soon as he got to know me, but if anything, all this time has done is confirm how right War is for me.

Any time I offered to give him space, he held me closer. He likes my bossy side and is the only man I've ever felt safe enough with to surrender.

I trust him.

Swallowing my pride, my fear, my doubts, I say, "War, this probably isn't the right time—"

The door slams open, and Tuesday and Bond rush in, silencing the question on the tip of my tongue. Tuesday throws her arms around War and catches sight of his bandaged bare feet.

"What did you do?"

When he doesn't answer, I do. "He showed that expensive timepiece who's boss." When all three heads in the room turn and look at me, I grimace. "Sorry. Ill-timed joke."

War cracks a grin and shakes his head. "I sure did."

I nudge him, encouraging him off the couch. Then I jerk my head toward the bar. "The note and, um, watch are up there."

There's a hushed gasp, and I meet Tuesday's tear-filled eyes as she holds the mangled remnants of War's watch. Bond, meanwhile, is a cloud of fury. He holds the thick linen paper like it's a filthy rag, his handsome face twisted in anger.

Tuesday pries the note from Bond's hand and what little color remaining in her cheeks bleeds away. "How could he... that bastard..." She paces back and forth in front of the bar, muttering.

Clearing my throat to get everyone's attention, I stand. "Why don't I let you guys talk about this in private." War goes to protest, but I give him a quick hug and kiss. "I'll go grab some breakfast. It's early, and I'm starving."

Bond nods. "That's a good idea. I'll call Clairy and give her a heads up."

I snag War's keys from the small hook by the door, but his hand on mine stops me.

"You don't have to leave, Trouble."

"I'm not leaving, at least not yet." He frowns at that. Cupping his cheek, I whisper, "You and your sister need time to talk. For now, I'm not leaving, but I am getting us a boatload of carbs and caffeine."

It's odd being in War's Bronco without him and weirder still driving around the streets of Trail Creek alone. Thankfully, the town is small enough that the handful of trips we've taken downtown from War's rental are enough for me to navigate to the bakery/cafe.

Clairy, bless her soul, waits for me outside The Bee and The Bean, three large white bags in hand. She sidles up to my window, smiling as she passes the bags to me.

"How are they?"

I hum and say, "In shock, I think."

"I've interacted with that awful man once, and that is one more than I'd wish on my worst enemy."

"On that, we can agree," I say as she passes me a drink carrier full of coffee.

When I return to War's, the mood is heavy, but not with despair; no, it's an air of determination. And I know from the set of War's jaw he won't be joining me in Pueblo.

My heart aches, but I stay busy unpacking the bags and passing out the coffee. Once they start eating, I slip from the living room.

> Think Jake can swing through Trail Creek and pick me up today?

DADDIO

> ...

I watch the dots bounce on my screen. Jake works for Dad and is hauling Xpresso up for the rodeo.

> Turns out Jake wasn't able to make the drive.
> X and I will be there in two hours.

Before I can call him, my phone buzzes in my hands again.

> We stayed the night in Dalhart and got an early start.
>
> Want to talk about what happened?

>> Thank you 🩶 There'll be plenty of time on the ride.

I flop on War's bed with a sigh and stare at the ceiling, willing my eyes to stay dry. This is the right thing to do. War needs time with Tuesday to figure this mess out. Even if they decide the answer is to do nothing, he should make that decision with her. Not over the phone or text because he's two hundred miles away with me.

A soft knock interrupts my mini pity party. War leans against the frame, his amber eyes searching over me. I crook a finger and pat the mattress. When he lays down next to me, I curl my body over his.

"I was going to ask you to come with me, but—"

"I was going to ask to go with you, but—"

His smile matches mine until our mouths are too busy for anything besides tasting each other. I savor these kisses. They'll have to last me a few days at least, possibly longer.

"How long do you have?" War asks, his large hands sliding under the hem of my tank top.

"Two hours. Is your sister still here?"

"No, she and Bond wanted to give us time to work out our next steps." His thumb grazes my nipple, and when it puckers under my shirt, War climbs on top of me and sucks it through the material.

"Mm, next steps?"

His teeth tug at the hardened peak, and my whimper spills into the room. "Yeah, Trouble. Next steps. I need a couple of days to square this mess up, but there's no way I'm letting you go to Pueblo without branding each inch of your body, all your delicious noises, into my brain. Or without a promise that I'll see you in the finals."

"Then I guess I'll let you do your worst, Pretty Boy."

Pleasure pulses between my legs at the teasing touch of War's fingers. With each kiss, each stroke, each thrust, the worry in my chest melts away, replaced with warm certainty.

We're going to be alright.

Cheyenne, Wyoming
April

X and I are on fire.

The Cheyenne Rodeo isn't as big of an event as Denver, but the pot tonight is nothing to blink at. Not to mention, a win here earns a heap of points. The big Boss and I are getting ready to warm up, and if all goes to plan, we're walking away as the queens tonight.

Night one was perfect, and night two followed suit. So long as I stay focused—and don't think about the silent phone I tucked away in my trailer—there's no doubt how things will play out.

War promised he'd be in Pueblo for the finals, but things

didn't go as planned. He didn't make it to Denver either. When he and Tuesday turned down their father's offer—shocking—they found several additional assets tied to family accounts they needed to clear out. He explained it all to me during one of the multi-hour video calls we shared during our time apart.

Morning chats are for sharing how we slept, what we have planned for the day. Mid-day is to check in on his and Tuesday's progress. Nights are for updates on how I raced, taking off our clothes, and pressing the boundaries of mutual masturbation.

Today, though, I only got my morning call. I'm trying not to pout, and I refrained from calling him after the first three went unanswered. I'm guessing something big is happening with the last holdings he and Tuesday are looking to liquidate.

Xpresso stamps her hoof, a prancy little move on her part to get my attention. Cooing to her, I take her lead and walk to the warm-up space. "We're winning tonight."

She tosses her glossy mane and nickers in agreement.

From behind me, a familiar voice chimes in. "Yep. You two are about to earn a big win. I can feel it."

"Hey, Dad, what are you doing back here?" I wave my arm, spurring him to catch up.

"Just checking on you." He flicks the brim of my hat.

I swat his hand away and straighten my Stetson. "We're good, and you're hovering. What's wrong?"

Dad holds his hands up in surrender. "Hovering? That makes me sound like your Memaw. You're breaking this old man's heart." At my smile and eye roll, he squeezes my shoulder. "Have a good run, Mimi. I'll be waiting for you after your victory lap."

X nudges me on, antsy to move. "I've got ya, girl. I'm ready to run, too."

There's no more time to think about War, Dad's weird

behavior, or anything else. By the time I work X through her warm-ups, they're calling me to the alley. Like always, I take a beat to center myself. All my favorite scents—minus War's body wash and skin—fill my nose. The mixture of hay, dirt, and horse soothes any remaining nerves, and with a pat to Xpresso's neck, we approach the gate.

The countdown clock flashes.

Five.

Four.

Three.

Two.

A toothy smile stretches across my face.

One.

And here we go.

Some people wait to change into a buckle they've won. Some never wear them at all. And some, the really cool ones, strip off their old buckle and slide the new one on the minute they jump off their horse.

I'm fiddling with my new hardware when a big hand settles on my lower back. Instantly, I know who it is. The bugs crawling up my spine are all the indication I need.

"Cyrus, get your goddamn hands off me."

"Easy, Lucky." His breath reeks, a mix of stale beer and gingivitis. The paw on my back shifts forward, sliding toward my hip. "Since you've already got your belt undone, why don't we—"

The words cut off, followed by a grunt and the sound of flesh hitting flesh. *Shit.* I spin, expecting to find my dad getting his butt kicked by Cyrus. Dad's a tough guy, but Cyrus is a scrapper with a lifetime of stupidity on his side.

My mouth drops when, instead of my fifty-year-old father, I see a handsome man with russet hair, a clean-shaven face, and the shoulders of a swimmer.

War pins Cyrus to the ground, his phone to his ear, as he grins at me. "Hey, sweetheart. I know you can handle yourself, but I've had enough of this guy."

I move to hug him, ready to lay him out in a full-body tackle but decide at the last second to drop my weight onto Cyrus' legs instead. Hugging War from behind, I ask, "What are you doing?"

"Here? Or right now?"

I stifle a laugh and bury my face in the soft flannel of his shirt. "Both."

War grunts and shifts, fighting to keep Cy on the ground. "Right now, I'm keeping this asshole from running off before security can get here. In general, I'm here to celebrate with the woman I lo—really like."

I'm about to correct him, to encourage him to say the rest of that first word. Love. Because I feel it, too. The last three weeks have been challenging, but it's also given us time to get to know each other. Fast? Sure. But also achingly slow.

A familiar pair of boots and two sets of dark combat-style shoes drift into my peripheral. I look up to find Dad and two security guards watching us. Dad quirks an eyebrow. "Should have known following these guys would lead me to you, Mimi."

I extend an arm and Dad pulls me to standing while the large uniformed men separate War and Cyrus. Pointing at the cowboy who once again attempted to ruin my night, I say, "He has a history of harassment. I have a complaint on file."

The security guard mumbles something into the radio on

his shoulder before nodding at me. They grip Cyrus' arms and lead him away; all the while, he's cussing and swearing and making an even bigger ass of himself.

As soon as they're out of sight, War has me in his arms. *This touch is welcome. So, so welcome.*

He presses a sweet kiss to my lips. "You kicked ass, Laramie. You and X were a well-oiled machine."

My cheeks heat with his compliment. "You saw me? I was worried you might be bad luck. The one race I knew you were there for was a disaster."

War throws back his head and laughs. *The way I want to lick this man's Adam's apple...*

"No way I'm bad luck. I watched you race live all three nights at Pueblo and Denver and for rounds one and two here."

"What?"

He tilts his head toward my dad, who shrugs and tucks his hands into his pockets. "You aren't the only one who knows how to video chat."

Every cell inside me combusts into a pile of goo. "You watched all my races?"

"Yep. Cheered for you, alongside Tuesday, Bond, and the rest. You've got a pretty big fan club in Trail Creek." He nuzzles his nose against mine until a cough from Dad pulls us apart.

"I'm flying to North Texas in the morning." He pats War on the back. "You're in good hands, Mimi."

"The best," I agree. "But you don't have to go. I've got a break before I have to be in Lincoln."

"I do have to get back. I've been gone for a longer stretch than usual, and the business and books are a mess."

War clears his throat. "About that... Would you want to spend your break at home?"

"Why would you want to go to Pilot Point? Isn't that a little close to Dallas for you?"

Dad smiles and shakes War's hand. "You two talk. See you soon, partner."

"Partner?" If I thought the biggest shock of the night was War's arrival in Wyoming, I'm sorely mistaken.

"Turns out Tuesday and I have some money to invest, and I've heard good things about the horses from Prairie Sky Equine and the owner." He gives me a salacious wink. "And the owner's daughter."

"You're investing in Dad's horses? Why?"

"It's a family business, isn't it?"

I nod.

"Well, I'm investing in my family."

Moving without thinking, I jump into War's arms. "I love you."

His eyes widen before fluttering shut, and his fingers tighten their grip. "I love you, too, Trouble."

"We've got a lot to—"

"We still have a lot to—"

We smile at each other. We have so much to learn, but we also have the rest of our lives to do it. I plop my hat onto his head and capture his mouth with mine because, really, what more is there to say?

epilogue

Las Vegas, Nevada
December

Eight months of traveling across the country. Thousands of miles. Dozens of rodeos. An infinite number of questionable bathrooms. All of it led us here.

Under the brightest lights in the world, I'm cheering on my Trouble as she makes her claim for the National Finals Rodeo crown. It's a sold-out crowd, and the energy is palpable. I down the ice-cold beer, the aluminum bottle crumpling in my grip. She's eighth tonight, and we're only on rider number four. I'm an old hat at rodeos and the anticipation of watching the love of my life ride now, but everything about tonight is heightened. All my years in the boardroom, dealing with million-dollar contracts and managing my father, have nothing on being in the stands waiting to see Laramie achieve her dream. It's a wholly different pressure. My leg bounces until Kit passes me another beer.

"Sip this one, Son."

"Yeah," Tuesday says. "You're making us nervous."

Kit, Bond, Tuesday, and the rest of the Trail Creek crew showed up a few days ago, sporting *Laramie Larson Fan Club: Trail Creek Branch* shirts. Each evening since, they've joined Kit and me in cheering for Laramie, always bringing matching tops for us all. Tonight, it's a hot pink sweatshirt my sister made that says ~~Lucky~~ *Laramie Larson: I'm not lucky; I'm talented.*

Tuesday grins and brushes off her shoulders. "This one's my favorite."

"I can't wait for her to see it." I already know how my girl will react. She'll fight back tears and make some smart-ass comment about how amazing she is, and then she'll take the shirt Tuesday gives her and carefully add it to the others. She's saving them all to get a quilt made.

The announcer's voice booms through the speakers, calling out the next rider's name and stats.

From next to me, Kit grunts. "She's good, but not as good as Mimi."

I hum my agreement. Truthfully, though, it doesn't matter if she comes in fifteenth or first; I'm so fucking proud of her. The format for the NFR differs from a lot of the smaller rodeos, so it's been a long ten days. Laramie's had great nights and ones where she and X didn't get the time they wanted, but overall, she's in excellent position for a top-five finish.

Riders five, six, and seven all put up commendable numbers. I've learned so much over the past eight months, like how to judge a race without even looking at the clock. I've also perfected the art of making Laramie fall apart on my fingers, tongue, and cock, but those skills aren't helpful right now.

Discreetly adjusting myself, I push last night's celebratory orgasm-fest from my mind and focus. It's time. With bated breath, I watch the countdown clock flash until it hits zero.

The thunder of hooves fills the arena, mixing with the roar

of the crowd to create a chaotic, frenzied symphony. Laramie and X move in perfect harmony, twin creatures of impulse and instinct. Together, they round the first barrel, Laramie trusting X with the certainty of someone born to ride.

She's glorious. Her long brown hair flies behind her, and those same strong thighs that rode me last night hold her trim body just inches off the saddle. Though I only catch flickers of her face, I know it's a mask of determination and joy.

I think about the second time I ever saw her, wrestling with a five-pound dumbbell, frustration pouring from her as she pushed through the pain. Later, in the hot tub, finding her underwater, my heart jumping into my throat, screaming at me to save her.

But in the end, she saved me. Sure, it was a rough road, but I wouldn't give up where I am now for anything.

The group around me lets out a collective sigh, followed by a series of exuberant whoops and woos. Laramie's time flashes on the jumbotron, the fastest of the night so far. I jump to my feet and push through the throngs of people until I reach the cordoned-off area separating the spectators from the athletes.

With all the confidence of a mediocre man who delusionally believes he's great—thanks for teaching me this one, Dad—I walk past security like I belong there. No one stops me, so I speed up, needing to wrap Laramie in my arms.

I search through the cacophony of horses, competitors, trainers, and more. I clench my teeth and flex my fingers. Laramie could be anywhere back here.

"Excuse me?" I stop a young man wearing a lanyard. "Can you point me toward the cool-down area?" He waves in a general direction, and I take off before he realizes I don't belong back here, as if my lack of boots and hat plus the bright pink sweatshirt with flowy script doesn't give me away.

The crowd thins as I move away from the gate, the energy

shifting from an urgent pressing to a soft hum. For a second, I worry I missed her somehow, but then, like my guiding beacon, I see her.

Laramie stands next to Xpresso, stroking her mane and whispering to her. No doubt, she's giving the Boss a treat and praising her for their run. My feet carry me forward until I'm pressing my face into her neck, breathing her in.

"Love you, Trouble."

With a laugh, she spins. "War!" Her eyes drop to my chest. "Oh, this one is my favorite so far!" Then she looks at me, a tiny crinkle forming between her eyebrows. "What are you doing back here?"

"Taking a page from your playbook and causing a little trouble."

Laramie's dark brown eyes radiate warmth and love as she smiles. "I'm a bad influence on you, Pretty Boy."

X snorts her agreement, and I reach around Laramie to pat the horse. "Hey Boss, I'm not taking her away till she's got you all taken care of, I promise."

"She's good. Watered and pepperminted. Now, it's just the waiting game." Laramie bites her lower lip and focuses on the screen. They're up to number eleven, and based on the cumulative average speeds, my girl is sitting in third.

"I keep trying not to look, but I can't seem to stop."

"Anything I can do to help?"

Laramie snags my hand and guides us until her back is against a nearby wall. She cranes her head, glancing to see if anyone is nearby. People linger in the area, but we're mostly hidden behind Xpresso and with the wall to our backs.

With a devilish grin, Laramie says, "Be a good boy and distract me."

I drop my head to her shoulder and groan. "Fuck, Trouble." My fingers grip her hips, kneading and squeezing them through the stiff material of her jeans. When she rises onto her tip-toes and settles her hat on my head, I know what she has in mind.

Despite all the blood rushing to my cock, I'm not looking for my release right now. No, my girl asked for a distraction, and I'm going to give her one. One hand slides up her back to her nape, collaring her. Her muscles instantly relax. As much as Laramie enjoys being in charge, she also drips when I take control.

I tilt her head back and kiss her. Taste her. Devour her. When she's pliant, I turn her until her cheek presses against the wall. My jaw tics with the need to slide my cock between her thighs, but there's not enough time. This has to be quick and dirty.

"Does my sweetheart want to ride my fingers? Do you need me to tease this pussy until you come?"

"Yes. Please!"

"Shhh, Laramie. We wouldn't want to draw a crowd." I thumb open the button of her jeans, then yank down the fly. Her Wranglers are so damn tight, I can hardly get my hand into them. But where there's a will...

Working slowly, I tease a finger through her curls and around her clit, loving the way she shivers. I kick her feet wider, giving myself more room to work. That single finger continues its exploration, dipping inside her up to the first knuckle before pulling out. Then I do it again, this time sinking deeper but still toying with her.

She squirms and huffs. "War, we don't have time—"

One finger becomes two, and I search and curl them inside her. With my free arm, I muffle her cries, my hips thrusting forward when she sinks her teeth into my forearm. The heel of my palm works her clit, giving her pressure outside, while inside, I work that sensitive spot that will make her shatter.

"Come for me, Trouble. I want to walk back out for the closing ceremonies with your scent on my hand, knowing you're sitting in drenched panties."

She whimpers my name, her knees giving out with her release. I grind my aching cock against her ass, doing what I can to take the edge off, but when she drops her head against my chest, her long lashes fluttering against her cheeks, and says, "I love you so fucking much, War," all my discomfort melts away.

"To Laramie!" Bond holds up a drink as we offer our cheers.

"To me!" she chirps, downing her third glass of champagne.

We're celebrating Laramie's fourth-place finish in a massive suite at some swanky hotel on the Strip. The final rider blazed through fast enough to bump her down a spot, but nothing but pride radiates from Laramie.

With her refilled glass in the air, she clears her throat. "Attention, please!"

The room turns to her, and of course, she preens. "Thank you all for being here this week, supporting me, and wearing all these amazing shirts." She gestures to the different tops behind her.

"You guys know us and our story. That we met in physical therapy, nursing shoulder injuries." Laramie steps into my arms and grins up at me. "*My* injury was from falling off a bronco and having surgery; a swimming pool brought War down." There's a round of laughter from our closest friends.

"You also know we had a rocky start." Her voice softens,

and she squeezes my arms where they rest around her waist. "I made a terrible mistake and hurt War. Then he pulled a me and ran." This earns her another small laugh. "His pain brought him to Trail Creek and you amazing people. And then, in a weird, wonderful twist, he ended up in Lubbock of all places.

"The War who showed up at the rodeo that night was nothing like the one I left in Dallas, and the biggest difference was—"

"The yeti beard!" Tuesday says.

"The overgrown hair?" Bond asks.

"The fifteen extra pounds?" This comes from me. I shrug and duck my head when everyone stares.

Laramie's bright giggle sounds around the room. "Those are all excellent guesses. But, no, the biggest difference was his spirit. He was softer, a little fragile, but undeniably someone I needed to know." She wiggles out of my grasp and crosses the room, digging through a bag. "And he also didn't have his watch."

My fingers absently rub my bare wrist, and I swallow back bitter bile at the memory of that stupid watch and all it symbolized. True to the word of his letter, neither Tuesday nor I have spoken with our parents since Warren Phillips, Sr. issued his ultimatum. But, I look around the room, we haven't wanted for family.

"Trouble, where are you going with this?"

She pushes me into an empty chair and climbs into my lap. "I have something for you."

There's a brick in my stomach as I take the clumsily wrapped box. It's cheap brown paper with printed horseshoes. Nothing like the last time I opened a box this size. There's no way it's another Breitling. Or, god forbid, the same damn one.

Laramie's lips brush my ear. "Don't worry, Pretty Boy, you'll like it."

I tear through the cheap paper, letting it fall to the floor. When I slide off the lid, there nestled on a bed of thin tissue paper lies a simple wooden watch. The face is dark brown, and it only tells time. No bells, no whistles. No gold casing or phases of the moon.

"Turn it over."

As I flip over the watch, my breath catches. Everyone else in the room disappears; it's just Laramie and me.

May you never go to battle without your wild horse.

I run a finger over the engraving and pull her face to mine. "Marry me."

Laramie jerks back. "What?"

Louder, I repeat the question. The one I need her to answer. "Will you marry me?"

Her mouth opens and closes as she nods, eyes wide and locked on mine.

"Need to hear you say it, sweetheart."

"Yes! Yes, I'll marry you!"

There's a rush of congratulations and well wishes, but I hear none. All I can see, smell, sense is her—my favorite kind of trouble.

dick-tionary

- Chapter 7: v/p scene between MCs
- Chapter 12: v/p scene between MCs, includes toy usage and anal play
- Chapter 14: v/p scene between MCs
- Epilogue: foreplay between MCs in a public location

acknowledgments

J and A thank you for making friendship bracelets, counting stickers, and keeping me fed. You two always cheer me on, even when I drag you to events and book stores.

Ellie, you are an amazing author and CP. And while I owe meeting you to the jankiest website ever, I will forever be an Ellie Mack stan.

To my Alphas, Cherry and Becky, thank you! For the brain dumps and the reassurance and just being amazing people.

To my betas, Hannah, Laura, Katie, Miley, and Tiff: thank you for your thoughts, feedback, and emoji reactions. You helped make this book better!

A huge massive thank you to the talented ladies in *The Smuttering*, who listen to me doubt myself and talk me out of deleting everything too many times to count. Thank you for making me laugh, providing visual treats, and being there when I need you. I am so thankful y'all let me tag along.

Tina, thank you for the last minute edit and always coming through!

My amazing ARC readers, I so appreciate you sharing your thoughts about Wild Horses out in the world.

To everyone who has recommended my books to others, come back for more, you have no idea how much it means to me.

Finally, to all of you, THANK YOU. From the bottom of my

heart, I hope you love the story, the characters, and the way they love each other.

about the author

Albany Archer is the alter ego of an avid reader—turned writer—of sweet and spicy romance. She loves anything with a happily ever after, regardless of the sub-genre. Banter, hair washing, and feisty female characters who know who and what they want are her love language. Her biggest hope is that you walk away with some sort of joy after reading her work.

If you'd like to connect with Albany, check out the links below.

- instagram.com/authoralbanyarcher
- goodreads.com/albanyarcher
- amazon.com/author/albanyarcher

also by albany archer

Davis Designs

Keep This Between Us

Wild Horses

(also part of the Sexy as Sin Series)

Brooks Brothers

Roughing It

Made in the USA
Columbia, SC
24 February 2025